JOKES TO KEEP YOU OCCUPIED DURING ISOLATION

J. J. Wilkinson

CONTENTS

INTRODUCTION

A selection of funny & (mostly) Awful jokes & One Liners to keep you amused whilst self isolating during the 2020 Covid 19 Pandemic.

All profits from this ebook will be used to help care workers who have put themselves on the frontline to keep the elderly safe.

REALLY BAD JOKES

I'm pretty much destined for greatness. I'm just pacing myself so I don't freak you out.

To steal ideas from one person is plagiarism; to steal from many is research.

"Crime in multi-storey car parks. That is wrong on so many different levels."

"When I was younger I felt like a man trapped inside a woman's body. Then I was born."

"I was playing chess with my friend and he said, 'Let's make this interesting'. So we stopped playing chess."

"I usually meet my girlfriend at 12:59 because I like that one-to-one time."

"I really wanted kids when I was in my early 20s but I could just never... lure them into my car. No, I'm kidding... I don't have a licence."

"I was very naive sexually. My first boyfriend asked me to do missionary and I buggered off to Africa for six months."

"One in four frogs is a leap frog."

"Love is like a fart. If you have to force it it's probably shit."

"I used to be addicted to swimming but I'm very proud to say I've been dry for six years."

"My grandad has a chair in his shower which makes him feel old, so in order to feel young he sits on it backwards like a cool teacher giving an assembly about drugs."

"My husband's penis is like a semi colon. I can't remember what it's for and I never use it anyway."

"I was raised as an only child, which really annoyed my sister."

"I bought myself some glasses. My observational comedy improved."

"You know you're working class when your TV is bigger than your book case."

"Most of my life is spent avoiding conflict. I hardly ever visit Syria."

"Life is like a box of chocolates. It doesn't last long if you're fat."

"I was thinking of running a marathon, but I think it might be too difficult getting all the roads closed and providing enough water for everyone."

"You can't lose a homing pigeon. If your homing pigeon doesn't come back, then what you've lost is a pigeon."

"My Dad said, always leave them wanting more. Ironically, that's how he lost his job in disaster relief."

"I wanted to do a show about feminism. But my husband wouldn't let me."

"One thing you'll never hear a Hindu say... 'Ah well, you only live once."

"My Dad told me to invest my money in bonds. So I bought 100 copies of Goldfinger."
"I've decided to stop masturbating, since then I've not really felt myself."

"My wife told me: 'Sex is better on holiday.' That wasn't a nice postcard to receive."

"The first time I met my wife, I knew she was a keeper. She was wearing massive gloves."

"As a kid I was made to walk the plank. We couldn't afford a dog."

"Money can't buy you happiness? Well, check this out, I bought myself a Happy Meal."

"My father was never sexist, he beat my brothers and I equally."

"The Scots invented hypnosis, chloroform and the hypodermic syringe. Wouldn't it just be easier to talk to a woman?"

"If you arrive fashionably late in Crocs, you're just late."

"I saw a documentary on how ships are kept together. Riveting!"

"I'm learning the hokey cokey. Not all of it. But – I've got the ins and outs."

"Today... I did seven press ups: not in a row."

"Stephen Hawking had his first date for 10 years last week. He came back, his glasses were smashed, he had a broken wrist, a twisted ankle and grazed knees; apparently she stood him up!"

"My friend got a personal trainer a year before his wedding. I thought: 'Bloody hell, how long's the aisle going to be'."

"Golf is not just a good walk ruined, it's also the act of hitting things violently with a stick ruined."

"Feminism is not a fad. It's not like Angry Birds. Although it does involve a lot of Angry Birds. Bad example."

"Oh my god, mega drama the other day: My dishwasher stopped working! Yup, his visa expired."

"'I think jokes about learning difficulties are OK so long as they're clever' is like saying 'I think jokes about blind people are OK so long as they're visual'"

"I just bought underwater headphones and it's made me loads faster. Do you know how motivating it is swimming to the theme song from Jaws? I mean my anxiety is through the roof but record times."

"I'm single. By choice. Her choice. No it was a mutual thing. We came to the mutual agreement that she would marry her ex boyfriend."

"My mother told me, you don't have to put anything in your mouth you don't want to. Then she made me eat broccoli, which felt like double standards."

"Red sky at night: shepherd's delight. Blue sky at night: day."

"It all starts innocently, mixing chocolate and Rice Krispies, but before you know it you're adding raisins and marshmallows – it's a rocky road."

"I was watching the London Marathon and saw one runner dressed as a chicken and another runner dressed as an egg. I thought: 'This could be interesting."

"The anti-ageing advert that I would like to see is a baby covered in cream saying, 'Aah, I've used too much'"
"Whenever I see a man with a beard, moustache and glasses, I think, 'There's a man who has taken every precaution to avoid people doodling on photographs of him'"

"Miley Cyrus. You know when she was born? 1992. I've got condiments in my cupboard older than that."

"'What's a couple?' I asked my mum. She said, 'Two or three'. Which probably explains why her marriage collapsed"

"My friend said she was giving up drinking from Monday to Friday. I'm just worried she's going to dehydrate"

"My granny was recently beaten to death by my grandad. Not as in, with a stick – he just died first"

"I think if you were hardcore anti-feminism, surely you wouldn't call yourself 'anti-feminism' would you? You'd call yourself 'Uncle Feminism'."

"I am writing a film script about going back in time to stop Hitler's parents meeting at the Austrian Enchantment 'Under The Sea' dance. It's called 'Back to the Fuhrer'!"

"My Mum was always saying that thing parents say growing up 'Wait until your dad gets home'. 'Wait until your dad gets home, we'll have a chat introduce you and see if he'll start paying maintenance'"

"I heard a rumour that Cadbury is bringing out an oriental chocolate bar. Could be a Chinese Wispa."

"I needed a password eight characters long so I picked Snow White and the Seven Dwarves."

"Crash Investigations is my favourite TV show, I've seen every episode. Here's a tip for the new viewers: if the show starts with the pilots being interviewed... it will be a boring episode."

"I think the bravest thing I've ever done is misjudge how much shopping I want to buy and still not go back to get a basket."

"Drug use gets an unfair reputation considering all the beautiful things in life it has given us like rock 'n' roll and sporting achievement."

"I'm not a very muscular man; the strongest thing about me is my password."

"I don't have the Protestant work ethic, I have the Catholic work ethic; in that I don't work but I do feel very guilty about that."

"I love Snapchat. I could talk about classic card games all day."

"People who use selfie sticks really need to have a good, long look at themselves."

"I think children are like Marmite. You either love them or you keep them at the back of the cupboard next to the piccalilli."

"Jokes about white sugar are rare. Jokes about brown sugar, Demerara."

"A rescue cat is like recycled toilet paper. Good for the planet, but scratchy."

"My cat is recovering from a massive stroke."

"My sister had a baby and they took a while to name her and I was like, 'Hurry up!' because I didn't want my niece to grow up to be one of these kids you hear about on the news where it says, 'The 17 year old defendant, who hasn't been named'."

"I've always considered myself more of a lover than a fighter. Which has confused a lot of guys that have tried to start fights with me. They'll raise their fists, I'll whip my knob out."

"I went to Waterstones and asked the woman for a book about turtles, she said 'hardback?' and I was like, 'yeah and little heads'"

"I learned about method acting at drama school, when all my classmates stayed in character as posh, patronising twats for the entire three years I was there."

"My ex-girlfriend would always ask me to text her when I got in. That's how small my penis is."

"Hey, if anyone knows how to fix some broken hinges, my door's always open."

"If you don't know what Morris dancing is, imagine eight guys from the KKK got lost, ended up at gay pride and just tried to style it out."

"Hedgehogs – why can't they just share the hedge?"

"I think the worst thing about driving a time machine is your kids are always in the back moaning 'Are we then yet?'"

"If you don't know what introspection is, you need to take a long, hard look at yourself."

"Insomnia is awful. But on the plus side – only three more sleeps till Christmas."

"I'm very conflicted by eye tests. I want to get the answers right but I really want to win the glasses."

"Relationships are like mobile phones. You'll look at your iPhone 5 and think, it used to be a lot quicker to turn this thing on."

Did you hear about the crook who stole a calendar? He got twelve months.

Q. What's the difference between ignorance and apathy? A. I don't know and I don't care.

Did you hear about the semi-colon that broke the law? He was given two consecutive sentences.

Never criticize someone until you've walked a mile in their shoes. That way, when you criticize them, they won't be able to hear you from that far away. Plus, you'll have their shoes.

The world tongue-twister champion just got arrested. I hear they're gonna give him a really tough sentence.

I own the world's worst thesaurus. Not only is it awful, it's awful.

So what if I don't know what "Armageddon" means? It's not the end of the world.

I woke up this morning and forgot which side the sun rises from, then it dawned on me.

Velcro – what a rip-off!

I recently decided to sell my vacuum cleaner as all it was doing was gathering dust.

Don't you hate it when someone answers their own questions? I do.

I hate Russian dolls, they're so full of themselves.

The best thing about good old days is that we were neither good nor old.

I have clean conscience. I haven't used it once till now.

If we shouldn't eat at night, why do they put a light in the fridge?

Moses had the first tablet that could connect to the cloud.

A lot of people cry when they cut onions. The trick is not to form an emotional bond.

I wrote a song about a tortilla. Well actually, it's more of a wrap.

Some people just have a way with words, and other people … oh … not have way.

The four most beautiful words in our common language: I told you so.

I bought one of those tapes to teach you Spanish in your sleep. During the night, the tape skipped. Now I can only stutter in Spanish.

My girlfriend and I often laugh about how competitive we are. But I laugh more.

Probably the worst thing you can hear when you're wearing a bikini is "Good for you!"

When I lost my rifle, the Army charged me £85. That's why in the Navy, the captain goes down with the ship.

A conference call is the best way for a dozen people to say "bye" 300 times.

When I was a boy, I had a disease that required me to eat dirt three times a day in order to survive... It's a good thing my older brother told me about it.

About a month before he died, my uncle had his back covered in lard. After that, he went down hill fast.

The first computer dates back to Adam and Eve. It was an Apple with limited memory, just one byte. And then everything crashed.

Alcohol is a perfect solvent: It dissolves marriages, families and careers.

Life without women would be a pain in the ass, literally.

A doctor tells a woman she can no longer touch anything alcoholic. So she gets a divorce.

I just asked my husband if he remembers what today is... Scaring men is easy.

I have never understood why women love cats. Cats are independent, they don't listen, they don't come in when you call, they like to stay out all night, and when they're home they like to be left alone and sleep. In other words, every quality that women hate in a man, they love in a cat.

My girlfriend is always stealing my t-shirts and sweaters... But if I take one of her dresses, suddenly "we need to talk".

Plan ahead - It wasn't raining when Noah built the ark.

To this day, the boy that used to bully me at school still takes my lunch money. On the plus side, he makes great Subway sandwiches.

Why did the blonde stare at a frozen orange juice can for 2 hours? Because it said "concentrate"!

I asked my North Korean friend how it was there, he said he

couldn't complain.

Behind every angry woman is a man who has absolutely no idea what he did wrong.

A diplomat is a man who always remembers a woman's birthday but never remembers her age.

She wanted a puppy. But I didn't want a puppy. So we compromised and got a puppy.

Women spend more time wondering what men are thinking than men spend thinking.

At what age is it appropriate to tell my dog that he's adopted?

Don't let your worries get the best of you; remember, Moses started out as a basket case.

I have noticed that everyone who is for abortion, has already been born.

According to most studies, people's number one fear is public speaking. Number two is death. Death is number two. Does that sound right? This means to the average person, if you go to a funeral, you're better off in the casket than doing the eulogy.

The dinner I was cooking for my family was going to be a surprise but the fire trucks ruined it.

Why do blondes have TGIF on their shoes? Toes go in first!

A blonde said, "I was worried that my mechanic might try to rip me off, I was relieved when he told me all I needed was indicator fluid."

My mom said that if I don't get off my computer and do my homework she'll slam my head on the keyboard, but I think she's jokinfjreoiwjrtwe4to8rkljreun8f4ny84c8y4t58lym4wthylmhawt4mylt4amlathnatyn

Photons have mass? I didn't even know they were Catholic.

My email password has been hacked. That's the third time I've had to rename the cat.

Letting the cat out of the bag is a whole lot easier than putting it back in.

Did you know that dolphins are so smart that within a few weeks of captivity, they can train people to stand on the very edge of the pool and throw them fish?

After the helicopter crash, the blond pilot was asked what happened. She replied, "It was getting chilly in there, so I turned the fan off."

Improve your memory by doing unforgettable things.

If you're going through Hell, keep going.

Ham and Eggs: A day's work for a chicken, a lifetime commitment for a pig.

My girlfriend was complaining last night that I never listen to her. Or something like that...

Before I tell my wife something important, I take both her hands in mine. That way she can't hit me with them.

Math Teacher: "If I have 5 bottles in one hand and 6 in the other hand, what do I have?"
Student: "A drinking problem."

What's your best non swearing insult? I hope you step on a lego.

You can make a water-bed more bouncy by using spring water.

Everything always ends well. If not – it's probably not the end.

A blonde heard that accidents happen close to home so she moved!

A man walks into a bar with a roll of tarmac under his arm and says: "Pint please, and one for the road."

What do you do if a blonde throws a grenade at you? Pull the pin and throw it back.

Why did the blonde scale the glass wall? To see what was on the other side.

Nurse: "We need a stool sample and a urine sample."
Man to wife: "What did she say?"
Wife to husband: "They want your underwear."

How do you get a blonde to marry you? Tell her she's pregnant.

My doctor told me I needed to break a sweat once a day so I told him I'd start lying to my wife.

Why is the day that you do laundry, cook, clean, iron and so on, called a day off?

I hate when I'm running on the treadmill for half an hour and look down to see it's been 4 minutes.

Entered what I ate today into my new fitness app and it just sent an ambulance to my house.

It was only when I bought a motorbike that I found out that adrenaline is brown.

How do you make a blonde laugh on Saturday? Tell her a joke on Wednesday!

I hope when I inevitably choke to death on gummy bears people just say I was killed by bears and leave it at that.

My girlfriend left me because she couldn't handle my OCD. I told her to close the door five times on her way out.

Two blondes fall down a well. One says to the other one, "Isn't it dark down here?" She replies, "I don't know. I can't see."

If you're not supposed to eat at night, why is there a light bulb in the refrigerator?

How many gays does it take to screw in a lightbulb? Two. One to screw it in and another to stand around and say 'FABULOUS!'

A friend is like a book: you don't need to read all of them, just pick the best ones.

Know what the hardest part of riding a scooter is? Telling your parents you're gay.

A healthy sleep not only makes your life longer, but also shortens the workday.

One day you're the best thing since sliced bread. The next, you're toast.

Smoking will kill you... Bacon will kill you... But, smoking bacon will cure it.

I'm not saying your perfume is too strong. I'm just saying the canary was alive before you got here.

I didn't fight my way to the top of the food chain to be a vegetarian.

I named my dog 6 miles so I can tell people that I walk 6 miles every single day.

Good health is merely the slowest possible rate at which one can die.

Intelligence is like an underwear. It is important that you have it, but not necessary that you show it off.

You take away the looks, money, intelligence, charm and success and, really, there's no real difference between me and George Clooney.

A computer once beat me at chess, but it was no match for me at kick boxing.

Light travels faster than sound. This is why some people appear bright until you hear them speak.

He slapped his two inches on the doctors desk. The doctor said "What is wrong with it?" "It's swollen."

Occasionally, a true friend gives his paw not his hand...

The problem with trouble shooting is that trouble shoots back.

I tried to explain to my 4-year-old son that it's perfectly normal to accidentally poop your pants, but he's still making fun of me.

A little boy asked his father, "Daddy, how much does it cost to get married?" Father replied, "I don't know son, I'm still paying."

How is it that I always seem to buy the plants without the will to live?

Feeling pretty proud of myself. The Sesame Street puzzle I bought said 3-5 years, but I finished it in 18 months.

I like having conversations with kids. Grownups never ask me what my third favorite reptile is.

When I told the doctor about my loss of memory, he made me pay in advance.

My wife made me a green hamburger today to celebrate St Patricks Day. I asked her how she colored it and she said she didn't know what I was talking about.

Moses was leading his people through the desert for 40 years. It seems, even in Biblical times men avoided asking the way.

I asked my wife if she ever fantasizes about me, she said yes - about me taking out the trash, mowing the lawn, and doing the dishes.

What did the blonde say when she found out she was pregnant? "Are you sure it's mine?"

Told my wife I wanted our kids every other weekend and she reminded me that we're married and live together so I'd have to see them every day.

If a man speaks in the forest and there is no woman there to hear it... is he still wrong?

Scientists say the universe is made up of Protons, Neutrons, and Electrons. They forgot to mention Morons.

I saw a sign that said "Watch for children" and I thought, "That sounds like a fair trade".

Never ask a woman who is eating ice cream straight from the carton how she's doing.

The older I get, the earlier it gets late.

Thanks for explaining the word "many" to me, it means a lot.

My wife just found out I replaced our bed with a trampoline; she hit the roof.

Always borrow money from a pessimist. He won't expect it back.

When my boss asked me who is the stupid one, me or him? I told him everyone knows he doesn't hire stupid people.

A woman's mind is cleaner than a man's: She changes it more often.

My wife says I can join your gang but I have to be home by 9.

I started out with nothing, and I still have most of it.

My girlfriend told me she was leaving me because I keep pretending to be a Transformer. I said, "No, wait! I can change."

I refused to believe my road worker father was stealing from his job, but when I got home, all the signs were there.

I like older men because they've gotten used to life's disappointments. Which means they're ready for me.

I bought some shoes from a drug dealer. I don't know what he laced them with, but I've been tripping all day.

Time waits for no man, time is obviously a woman.

My kids are at an age now where they are beginning to understand embarrassment. This is my time to shine.

My IQ came back negative.

Sometimes the best helping hand you can give is a good, firm push.

Walking my dog we saw a guy in a suit walking his dog and I know my dog is thinking I don't dress nice for him anymore.

I always feel better when my doctor says something is normal for my age but then think dying will also be normal for my age at some point.

So apparently RSVP'ing back to a wedding invite 'maybe next time' isn't the correct response.

My therapist says I have a preoccupation with vengeance. We'll see about that.

When wearing a bikini, women reveal 90 % of their body... men are so polite they only look at the covered parts.

My wife says she is no longer buying junk food for the family because, "Everyone just eats it."

Artificial intelligence is no match for natural stupidity.

A woman says to the dentist "I don't know which is worse having a tooth pulled or having a Baby."
The dentist says "Well make up your mind I gotta adjust the chair!"

My son asked me what it's like to be married so I told him to leave me alone and when he did I asked him why he was ignoring me.

Nothing is fool proof to a sufficiently talented fool.

Being an adult is just walking around wondering what you're forgetting.

A recent study has found that women who carry a little extra weight live longer than the men who mention it.

That awkward moment when you leave a store without buying anything and all you can think is "act natural, you're innocent".

I organized a threesome last night. There were a couple of no-shows, but I still had fun.

I asked God for a bike, but I know God doesn't work that way. So I stole a bike and asked for forgiveness

Remember, if you smoke after sex you're doing it too fast.

You know you're ugly when it comes to a group picture and they hand you the camera.

I tried to be polite and hold the door open for a woman, but she kept screaming, "I'm peeing in here!"

The early bird might get the worm, but the second mouse gets the cheese.

A bank is a place that will lend you money, if you can prove that you don't need it.

If a quiz is quizzical, then what does that make a test?

A big shout out to pavements... Thanks for keeping me off the streets.

I don't have a girlfriend, I just know a girl who would get really mad if she heard me say that.

Whatever you do in life, always give 100%. Unless you're donating blood...

Sex is not the answer. Sex is the question. "Yes" is the answer.

Buying a smart car seems like a good idea until you hit a squirrel and flip over a few times.

The big difference between sex for money and sex for free is that sex for money usually costs a lot less.

Someone should open up a restaurant called "I don't care". Then we can finally go to that restaurant my girlfriends always talking about

I just read an article about the dangers of drinking that scared the crap out of me. That's it. No more reading!

I saw a woman wearing a sweat shirt with "Guess" on it...so I said "Implants?"

Women might be able to fake orgasms. But men can fake a whole relationship.

Honesty may be the best policy, but it's important to remember that apparently, by elimination, dishonesty is the second-best policy

It's funny how axe handles are made of wood. It's like the ultimate 'F*ck you' to trees.

Men have two emotions: Hungry and Horny. If you see him without an erection, make him a sandwich

It's so cold outside, I actually saw a gangster pull his pants up.

Never make an arm wrestling bet with a man that has been single for longer than 6 months.

Men are like babies... when they get cranky, just shove a nipple in their mouth!

Having sex is like playing bridge. If you don't have a good partner, you'd better have a good hand.

If you are supposed to learn from your mistakes, why do some people have more than one child.

Knowledge is knowing a tomato is a fruit; Wisdom is not putting it in a fruit salad.

If you think nobody cares if you're alive, try missing a couple of payments.

Children: You spend the first 2 years of their life teaching them to walk and talk. Then you spend the next 16 years telling them to sit down and shut-up.

If 4 out of 5 people SUFFER from diarrhea, does that mean that one enjoys it?

What should you give a man who has everything? A mute nymphomaniac 18 year old girlfriend.

You are such a good friend that if we were on a sinking ship together and there was only one life jacket, I'd miss you heaps and think of you often.

What's the difference between a new husband and a new dog? After a year, the dog is still excited to see you.

Behind every successful man is his woman. Behind the fall of a successful man is usually another woman.

Some people say "If you can't beat them, join them" I say "If you can't beat them, beat them", because they will be expecting you to join them, so you will have the element of surprise.

What is the thinnest book in the world? Biographies of Happy women.

My psychiatrist told me I was crazy and I said I want a second opinion. He said okay, you're ugly too.

I always take life with a grain of salt, plus a slice of lemon, and a shot of tequila.

Join The Army, visit exotic places, meet strange people, then kill them.

When you go into court, you are putting your fate into the hands of people who weren't smart enough to get out of jury duty.

Why do they lock gas station bathrooms? Are they afraid someone will clean them?

The difference between in-laws and outlaws? Outlaws are wanted.

I have all the money I'll ever need, if I die by 4:00 p.m. today.

Isn't it odd the way everyone automatically assumes that the goo in soap dispensers is always soap? I like to fill mine with mustard, just to teach people a lesson in trust.

I have a lot of growing up to do. I realized that the other day inside my fort.

An escalator can never break, it can only become stairs.

The worst time to have a heart attack is during a game of charades

I had a wonderful childhood, which is tough because it's hard to adjust to a miserable adulthood.

One day I ran into my girlfriend with my car. She asked me why I didn't ride around her. I told her that I didn't think I had enough petrol

Why are husbands like lawn mowers? They're hard to get started, emit foul odors, and don't work half the time.

What do men and beer bottles have in common? They're both empty from the neck up.

I had some words with my wife, and she had some paragraphs with me.

A consensus means that everyone agrees to say collectively what no one believes individually

Two blondes fell down a hole. One said, "It's dark in here isn't it?" The other replied, "I don't know; I can't see."

A cross eyed teacher couldn't control his pupils.

Never trust atoms, they make up everything.

After the accident, the juggler didn't have the balls to do it.

When you dream in color, it's a pigment of your imagination.

Want to hear a pizza joke? Never mind, it's too cheesy.

What do you call a fake noodle? An impasta.

To learn about paranoids, follow them around.

Did you hear about the guy whose whole left side was cut off? He's all right now.

When they bought a water bed, the couple started to drift apart

A bicycle can't stand alone because it is two-tired.

A cardboard belt would be a waist of paper.

Whiteboards are remarkable.

Why did the tomato turn red? Because it saw the salad dressing.

Energizer Bunny arrested, charged with battery.

What grows up while growing down? A goose.

A chicken crossing the road is poultry in motion.

What's the definition of a will? - Come on, it's a dead giveaway!

What do you call a Spanish pig? Porque.

The math professor went crazy with the blackboard. He did a number on it.

Corduroy pillows are making headlines.

I'd tell you a chemistry joke but I know I wouldn't get a reaction

"Waiter! This coffee tastes like mud." "Yes sir, it's fresh ground."

Why did the little fella sleep on the chandelier? Because he was a light sleeper.

Did you hear about the guy who got hit in the head with a can of soda? He was lucky it was a soft drink.

Tried to play my shoehorn - all I got was footnotes

People who say they suffer from constipation are full of crap.

Towels can't tell jokes. They have a dry sense of humor.

If Apple made a car, would it have Windows?

What did the chimpanzee say when his sister had a baby? Well, I'll be a monkey's uncle.

He had a photographic memory which was never developed.

So what if I don't know what Armageddon means? It's not the end of the world

The man who fell into an upholstery machine is fully recovered.

Don't use a big word where a diminutive one will suffice

Organized people are simply too lazy to search for stuff.

My neighbors are listening to great music. Whether they like it or not.

If you had to decide between a diet and a piece of chocolate, would you prefer dark, white or milk chocolate?

Sometimes I drink water - just to surprise my liver.

My mother never saw the irony of calling me a Son-of-a-bitch

I am nobody. Nobody is perfect. I am perfect.

If a problem can be solved then there's no use worrying about it, but if a problem can't be solved then what's the use of worrying

I am not saying kill all the stupid people, just get rid of the warning labels and let the problem sort itself out

Remember, you are absolutely unique. Just like everybody else.

I dream of a world where chickens can cross the road without having their motives questioned.

As long as cocoa beans grow on trees, chocolate is fruit to me.

Finally, the spring is here! I'm so thrilled I wet my plants.

The perfect man doesn't swear, doesn't smoke, doesn't get angry, doesn't drink. He also doesn't exist.

Stressed is just desserts spelled backwards.

I'm all for irony, but the phrase "Good morning" seems to be going a bit too far.

Time is the best teacher, Unfortunately it kills all its students!

I have often wanted to drown my troubles, but I can't get my wife to go swimming.

Go bungee jumping. Your life started with a malfunctioning rubber, so it's only right it should end that way, too.

I like to be an optimist. It pisses people off.

They say crime doesn't pay. So does my current job make me a criminal?

Money alone won't make you happy. You've got to own it.

The nine most terrifying words in the English language are, 'I'm from the government and I'm here to help.

Find out what you like doing best and get someone to pay you for doing it.

I'm not lazy. I'm just naturally a very relaxed person.

I'm standing outside. In other words, I'm outstanding.

Alcohol does not solve any problems, but then again, neither does milk.

My girlfriend told me to go out and get something that makes her look sexy... so I got drunk.

I'm not a strict vegetarian, I eat beef and pork.

My wallet is like an onion. Opening it makes me cry.

When a woman says "what?" It's not because she didn't hear you. She's just giving you a chance to change what you said.

QUESTION & ANSWER TIME

Q: What do you call a boomerang that won't come back?
A: A stick.

Q: What do you call a clairvoyant midget who just broke out of prison?
A: A small medium at large.

Q: What's the best thing about having Alzheimer's Disease?
A: You can hide your own easter eggs.

Q: What's the difference between 'Oooh' and 'Aaah'?
A: About 3 inches

Q: How do you know if a blonde has been sending e-mail?
A: You see a bunch of envelopes stuffed into the disk drive.

Q: What do breasts and martinis have in common?

A: One is not enough and three are too many.

Q: What do you call a row of rabbits jumping backwards?
A: A receding hair line.

Q: What's 50' long and smells of urine?
A: A line dance at a retirement village.

Q: What's the difference between erotic and kinky?
A: Erotic is when you use a feather. Kinky is when you use the whole chicken.

Q: What is the best definition of a mixed emotion?
A: Watching the mother-in-law reverse off a cliff driving your brand new car.

Q: What is the ultimate rejection?
A: When you're masturbating and your hand falls asleep.

Q: What is a man's view of safe sex?
A: A padded head board.

Q: What's green and smells like pork?
A: Kermit the Frog's finger.

Q: Why is divorce so expensive?
A: Because it's worth it

Q: What's the difference between light and hard?
A: You can sleep with a light on.

Q: Why do men find it difficult to make eye contact?
A: Because breasts don't have eyes

Q: What happens if you sing country music backwards?
A: You get your job and your wife back.

Q: How do porcupines make love?
A: Veerry carefully!

Q: What's the difference between a girlfriend and a wife?
A: 45 lbs.

Q: Whats a mans idea of foreplay?
A: Half hour of begging.

Q: How do you piss your wife off when you're making love?
A: Phone her!

Q: Why don't blind people like to sky dive?
A: Because it scares the hell out of the seeing eye dog.

Q: What's the difference between a boyfriend and a husband?
A: 45 minutes.

Q: What do you do when the dishwasher quits working?
A: Slap her.

Q: What's the difference between a blonde and a brick?
A: When you lay a brick, it doesn't follow you around for two weeks whining.

Q: Why do most married men die before their wives?
A: Because they want to.

Q: How many men does it take to screw in a light bulb?
A: One ... men will screw anything.

Q: What did the cannibal get when he was late for dinner?
A: The cold shoulder.

Q: What's the fastest way to a man's heart?
A: Through his chest with a sharp knife.

Q: What is another name for female Viagra?
A: A Diamond

Q: What do you do with 365 used rubbers?
A: Melt them down, make a tire, and call it a Goodyear.

Q: What's the difference between Princess Diana and Tiger Woods?
A: Tiger Woods had a better driver!

Q: What do you get from a pampered cow?
A: Spoiled milk

Q: Why do gorillas have big nostrils?
A: Because they have big fingers.

Q: What is the thinnest book in the world?
A: "What Men Know About Women."

Q. Why do black widow spiders kill their males after mating?
A. To stop the snoring before it starts.

Q. Why don't men have mid-life crises?
A. They stay stuck in adolescence.

Q. What's the difference between men and government bonds?
A. Bonds mature.

Q. What did the guy say to his dick after he found that the girl he's getting ready to fuck has genital warts?
A. "Hang on, boy! It's gonna be a bumpy ride!"

Q. Why does it take longer to build a blond snowman?
A. Because you have to hollow the head out.

Q. What is the only game in which the more you lose, the more you have to show for it?
A. Strip Poker

Q. What did the boy vampire say to the girl vampire?
A. See you next period.

Q. What's the hardest thing about a sex change operation?
A. Inserting the anchovies.

Q. What do you do in case of fallout?
A. Put it back in and take shorter strokes.

Q. What is the definition of a perfect lover?
A. A man with a nine inch tongue who can breath through his ears.

Q. What do you call an intelligent, good looking, sensitive man?
A. A rumor

Q. Why do you never see chicken in underwear?
A. Because their peckers are on their face.

Q. What's the difference between a girlfriend and wife?
A. 45 lbs.

Q. Why does a dog lick its penis?
A. Because it can't make a fist.

Q. How do you teach a blond math?
A. Subtract her clothes, divide her legs, and square root her.

Q. What's the last thing Tickle Me Elmo receives before he leaves the factory?
A. Two test tickles

Q. Why did God create alcohol?
A. So ugly people would have a chance to have sex.

Q. What is it when a man talks dirty to a woman?
A. Sexual harassment.

Q. What is it when a woman talks dirty to a man?
A. £3.99 a minute.

Q. What's the speed limit of sex?
A. 68 because at 69 you have to turn around.

Q. What's the ultimate rejection?
A. When you're masturbating and your hand falls asleep.

Q. What's worse then 10 dead babies nailed to one tree?
A. One dead baby nailed to 10 trees

Q. why did Humpty Dumpty push his girlfriend on the wall?
A. To see her crack

Q. What is the difference between great literature and pornog-

raphy?
A. Literature is frequently dusty but rarely dirty.

Q. Why does a squirrel swim on its back?
A. To keep its nuts dry.

Q. Why was Tigger's head in the toilet?
A. He was looking for pooh!

Q. How do you make a snooker table laugh.
A. Put your hands in its pocket and tickle its balls.

Q. What does Popeye do to keep his favorite tool from rusting?
A. Sticks it in Olive Oyl.

Q. What's a diaphragm?
A. A trampoline for dickheads.

Q. What proof do we have that prostitution is recession-proof?
A. Everyone knows that hookers thrive on hard times.

Q. What do a dildo and soy beans have in common?
A. They are both used as substitute meat.

Q. What do you call a man who cries while he masturbates?
A. A tearjerker.

Q. What's the difference between medium and rare?
A. 6 inches is medium, 8 inches is rare.

Q. How is a woman like a road?
A. Both have manholes.

Q. What do you call twelve naked men sitting on each others shoulders?
A. A scrotum pole!

Q. How many women with PMS does it take to screw in a light bulb?
A. One. ONE!! And do you know WHY it only takes ONE? Because no one else

in this house knows HOW to change a light bulb. They don't even know the

bulb is BURNED OUT. They would sit in this house in the dark for THREE DAYS

before they figured it OUT. And once they figured it out they wouldn't be

able to find the light bulbs despite the fact that they've been in the SAME

CUPBOARD for the past SEVENTEEN YEARS. But if they did, by some miracle, find

the light bulbs, TWO DAYS LATER the chair that they dragged from two rooms over

to stand on to change the STUPID light bulb would STILL BE IN THE SAME SPOT!!!!!!!

AND UNDERNEATH IT WOULD BE THE CRUMPLED WRAPPER THE STUPID LIGHT BULBS CAME IN. WHY???

BECAUSE NO ONE IN THIS HOUSE EVER CARRIES OUT THE GARBAGE!!!! IT'S A WONDER WE

HAVEN'T ALL SUFFOCATED FROM THE PILES OF GARBAGE THAT ARE 12 FEET DEEP THROUGHOUT

THE ENTIRE HOUSE. THE HOUSE!! THE HOUSE!!! IT WOULD TAKE AN ARMY TO CLEAN THIS...

Q. What do a Rubix cube and a penis have in common?
A. The longer you play with them, the harder they get.

Q. What is the difference between a woman and a washing machine?
A. You can bung your load in a washing machine and it won't call you a week later.

Q. Why did god create Adam before he created eve?
A. Because he didn't want anyone telling him how to make Adam.

Q. What did the elephant say to the naked man?
A. "How do you breath through something so small?"

Q. Why don't women wear watches?

A. There's a clock on the stove!

Q. What doesn't belong in this list : Meat, Eggs, Wife, Blowjob?
A. Blowjob: You can beat your meat, eggs or wife, but you can't beat a blowjob.

Q. Have you heard about the new super-sensitive condoms?
A. They hang around after the man leaves and talks to the woman.

Q. What's worse than getting raped by Jack the Ripper?
A. Getting fingered by Captain Hook.

Q. What do a walrus and Tupperware have in common?
A. They both like a tight seal.

Q. What's the difference between a wife and a wheelie bin?
A. You only have to take out a wheelie bin once a week.

Q. What did the two lesbian frogs say to each other?
A. WE DO TASTE LIKE CHICKEN!

Q. What did the banana say to the vibrator?
A. Why are you shaking she's going to eat me.

Q. What would happen if the Pilgrims had killed cats instead of turkeys?
A. We'd eat pussy every Thanksgiving.

Q. What's the difference between love and herpes?
A. Love doesn't last forever.

Q. How do you make your girlfriend scream while having sex?
A. Call her and tell her.

Q. Why do women have small feet?
A. So they can stand closer to the kitchen sink.

Q. Why do men die before their wives?
A. They want to.

Q. How do men sort out their laundry?
A. Filthy, and filthy but wearable.

Q. What's the difference between a man and ET?
A. ET phoned home.

Q. Why haven't they sent a woman to the moon yet?
A. It doesn't need cleaning.

Q. What's the difference between your paycheck and your cock?
A. You don't have to beg your wife to blow your paycheck!

Q. What do you call kids born in whorehouses?
A. Brothel sprouts.

Q. What's the difference between a 40 year-old man, and a 40 year-old woman?
A. A 40 year-old woman dreams of having children, a 40 year-old man dreams of dating them.

Q. What's white, smells, and can be found in panties?
A. Clitty litter

Q. Why is psychoanalysis quicker for men than for women?
A. When it's time to go back to his childhood, he's already there.

Q. Did you hear about the constipated mathematician?
A. He worked it out with a pencil.

Q. Who's the world's greatest athlete?
A. The guy who finishes first and third in a masturbation contest.

Q. Why do men pay more for car insurance?
A. Women don't get blow jobs while they're driving

Q. Three words to ruin a man's ego...
A. "Is it in?"

Q. How does a guy know if he has a high sperm count?
A. If the girl has to chew, before she swallows.

Q. What's in the toilet of the star ship enterprise?
A. The captains log.

Q. What do you call a woman with her tongue sticking out?
A. A lesbian with a hard-on.

Q. Did you hear they came out with a new lesbian shoe?
A. They're called Dikes. They have an extra long tongue and only take one finger to get off!

Q. What's the difference between tampons and cowboy hats?
A. Cowboy hats are for ass holes.

Q. What do you say to a virgin when she sneezes?
A. Goes-in-tight!

Q. How do you know when you are getting old?
A. When you start having dry dreams and wet farts.

Q. What's the definition of a Yankee?
A. Same thing as a "quickie", only you do it yourself.

Q. Why don't little girls fart?
A. Because they don't get assholes until they're married.

Q. Why do women stop bleeding when entering the menopause ?
A. Because they need all the blood for their varicose veins!

Q. What do Disney World & Viagra have in common?
A. They both make you wait an hour for a two minute ride.

Q. What's the definition of trust?
A. Two cannibals giving each other a blowjob.

Q. Why is it called a Wonder Bra?
A. When she takes it off, you wonder where her tits went.

Q. Why don't women blink during foreplay?
A. They don't have time.

Q. Why does it take 1 million sperm to fertilize 1 egg?
A. They don't stop for directions.

Q. Barking dog at the back door wanting in and your wife's yelling

at the front wanting in. Which one do you let in?
A. The dog, once he's in, he shuts up!

Q. How do you know when your wife is really dead?
A. Your sex life is the same but your washing pile gets bigger.

Q. How do you turn a fox into an elephant
A. Marry it.

Q. How do you make five pounds of fat look good?
A. Give it a nipple.

Q. What do you call two lesbians in a canoe?
A. Fur traders.

Q. What do you call a virgin on a waterbed?
A. A cherry float.

Q. How did Pinocchio find out he was made of wood?
A. When his hand caught on fire.

Q. What did Adam say to Eve?
A. Stand back, I don't know how big this thing gets!

Q. How do you get a nun pregnant?
A. Dress her up as an alter boy

Q. Why don't witches wear panties when flying on their broomsticks?
A. Better traction.

Q. What does parsley and pubic hair have in common?
A. Push it aside and keep on eating...

Q. Why is a woman's pussy like a warm toilet seat?
A. They both feel good, but you wonder who was there before you.

Q. What is the first sign of AIDS?
A. A pounding sensation in the ass.

Q. What did Cinderella do when she got to the ball?

A. Gagged

Q. What is the Difference Between Pussy and Apple Pie?
A. You can eat your mom's apple pie.

Q. Why do women pierce their bellybutton?
A. Place to hang their air freshener.

Q. Did you hear Cher is joining the spice girls?
A. They're going to call her Old Spice.

Q. What is the difference between a clever midget and a venereal disease?
A. One is a cunning runt, and the other is a running cunt

Q. What's the difference between oral sex and anal sex?
A. Oral sex makes your day, anal sex makes your hole weak.

Q. What do women and police cars have in common?
A. They both make a lot of noise to let you know they are coming.

Q. Why do female skydivers wear jock straps?
A. So they don't whistle on the way down.

Q. Why did the woman cross the road?
A. Never mind that, what the fuck is she doing out of the kitchen?

Q. Why do women have 2% more brains then a cow?
A. So, when you pull their tits they won't shit on the floor.

Q. Why can't women read maps?
A. Because only the male mind can comprehend the concept of 1 inch equals a mile.

Q. What's a virgin and a balloon have in common?
A. All it takes is one prick and its all over.

Q. What's the difference between your wife and your job?
A. After five years your job will still suck.

Q. What do you get when you cross a rooster and peanut butter?
A. A cock that sticks to the roof of your mouth.

Q. Why do women prefer old gynaecologists?
A. Their shaky hands!

Q. What is better than a cold Bud?
A. A warm bush.

Q. What do you do if your girlfriend starts smoking?
A. Slow down and use some lubricant.

Q. Why are women like Kentucky Fried Chicken?
A. After you've finished with the thigh and breasts, all you have left is a greasy box to put your bone in.

Q. What does a bull do to stay warm on a bitterly cold day?
A. He goes into the barn and slips into a nice warm "Jersey"

Q. What do you call an open can of tuna in a lesbians apartment?
A. Potpourri

Q. How are women and linoleum floors alike?
A. You lay them right the first time and you can walk all over them for the next 20 years.

Q. How are a lawyer and a prostitute different?
A. The prostitute stops fucking you after you're dead.

Q. What is a zebra?
A. 26 sizes larger than an "A" bra.

Q. What did the blind man say as he passed the fish market?
A. Good morning Girls

Q. What's the difference between a woman and a fridge?
A. A fridge doesn't fart when you pull your meat out!

Q. How is being at a singles bar different than being at the circus?
A. At the circus, the clowns don't talk.

Q. Why do men find it difficult to make eye contact?
A. Breasts don't have eyes.

Q. How many newspapers can a woman hold between her legs?
A. One Post, two Globes, and many Times.

Q. What's the difference between a whore and a bitch?
A. Whore's fuck everyone at the party, Bitches fuck everyone at the party except you.

Q. Did ya hear about the new "morning after" pill for men?
A. It works by changing your blood type!!

Q. What do you call a truck full of dildos?
A. Toys for Twats

Q. How do you get four old ladies to shout "Fuck"?
A. Get a fifth old lady to shout "Bingo!"

Q. What's the difference between a new husband and a new dog?
A. After a year, the dog is still excited to see you.

Q. What is the difference between a female snowman and a male snowman?
A. Snowballs.

Q. How many men does it take to open a beer bottle?
A. None It should be open when she brings it to you

Q. What's the difference between pink and purple?
A. The grip!

Q. What do you call it when a 90 year old man masturbates successfully?
A. Miracle whip.

Q. What's the definition of macho?
A. Jogging home from your own vasectomy.

Q. What do a clitoris, an anniversary, and a toilet have in common?
A. Men always miss them.

Q. What does do women and milk cartons have in common?

A. You gotta open the flaps to get to the good stuff.

Q. Why do bunnies have soft sex?
A. They have cotton balls

Q. What happens when you kiss a canary?
A. You get chirpes, it can't be tweeted because its a canarial disease.

Q. What does the receptionist at the sperm clinic say to clients as they are leaving?
A. Thanks for coming.

Q. What do a gynaecologist and a pizza delivery boy have in common?
A. They can both smell it, but can't eat it.

Q. You know why they say that eating oysters will improve a man's sex life?
A. Because women know if he'll eat one of those, he'll eat anything!

Q. Why does a bride smile when she's walking down the aisle?
A. She knows she's given her last blow job.

Q. Why is the space between a woman's breasts and her hips called a waist?
A. Because you could easily fit another pair of tits in there.

Q. What is the definition of "making love"?
A. Something a woman does while a guy is fucking her.

Q. What's the only animal with an asshole in the middle of its back?
A. A police horse.

Q. What does it mean when the flag at the Post Office is flying at half mast?
A. They're hiring.

Q. Did you hear Richard Simmons had plastic surgery to get his

love handles removed?
A. Yeah...now he has no ears.

Q. Do you know how to eat a frog?
A. You put one leg over each ear.

Q. How are fat girls and mopeds alike?
A. They are fun to ride but you don't want your friends to find out.

Q. How do you fuck a fat chick?
A. Roll her in flour and find the wet spot.
Q. What's the difference between a new husband and a new dog.
A. After a year, the dog is still excited to see you.

Q. Why is sleeping with a man like a soap opera?
A. Just when it's getting interesting, they're finished until next time.

Q. What do you call a guy who never farts in public?
A. A private tutor.

Q. What do you call a musician without a girlfriend?
A. Homeless.

Q. What has 2 grey legs and 2 brown legs?
A. An elephant with diarrhea.

Q. Why did the Avon lady walk funny?
A. Her lipstick

Q. What does the cannibal do just after he dumped his girlfriend?
A. Wiped his ass.

Q. What is the smallest hotel in the world?
A. A pussy, cause you have to leave the bags outside.

Q. What do a toilet and a woman have in common?
A. Without the hole in the middle they aren't good for shit.

Q. How can you tell a tough lesbian bar?
A. Even the pool table has no balls.

Q. How do you find a blind man in a nudist colony?
A. It's not hard.

Q. What do you call a lesbian with fat fingers?
A. Well hung.

Q. What two words will clear out a men's changing room quicker than anything else?
A. Nice dick!

Q. How do you know when a Barbie has her period?
A. All your tic tacks are gone.

Q. How do you know when you honeymoon is over?
A. When he no longer smiles as he scrapes the burnt toast

Q. What do a gynaecologist and a pizza delivery boy have in common?
A. They can both smell it, but can't eat it.

Q. You know why they say that eating oysters will improve a man's sex life?
A. Because women know if he'll eat one of those, he'll eat anything!

Q. Why does a bride smile when she's walking down the aisle?
A. She knows she's given her last blow job.

Q. Why is the space between a woman's breasts and her hips called a waist?
A. Because you could easily fit another pair of tits in there.
Q. What's the only animal with an asshole in the middle of its back?
A. A police horse.

Q. What does it mean when the flag at the Post Office is flying at half mast?
A. They're hiring.

Q. Did you hear Richard Simmons had plastic surgery to get his

love handles removed?
A. Yeah...now he has no ears.

Q. Do you know how to eat a frog?
A. You put one leg over each ear.

Q. How are fat girls and mopeds alike?
A. They are fun to ride but you don't want your friends to find out.

Q. What is the lightest thing in the world?
A. A penis...even a thought can raise it.

Q. What do gay kids get for Christmas?
A. Erection Sets.

Q. Where do fags park?
A. In the rear.

Q. Difference between a man buying a lottery ticket and a man fighting with his wife...
A. A man has a chance at winning at the lottery.

Q. What does a female snail say during sex?
A. Faster, faster, faster!

Q. What is the noisiest thing in the world?
A. Two skeletons screwing on a tin roof.

Q. What's red and blue with a long string?
A. A smurfette with her period.

Q. What do you call an adolescent rabbit?
A. A pubic hair.

Q. Define "Egghead:"
A. What Mrs. Dumpty gives to Humpty.

Q. How can you tell if you have acne?
A. If the blind can read your face.

Q. Did you know they just discovered a new use for sheep in New Zealand?

A. Wool!

Q. What's a necrophiliac's biggest complaint about sex?
A. They just kinda lay there.

Q. What did the woman say to her swimming instructor?
A. "Will I really drown if you take your finger out?"

Q. Why did the lumber truck stop?
A. To let the lumber jack off.
Q. Why did the woman get thrown out of the riding stable?
A. She wanted to mount the horse her way.

Q. Hey, what's sticky, white and falls from the sky?
A. The cumming of the Lord

Q. How did the tugboat get AIDS?
A. It was rear-ended by a ferry.

Q. How can you tell a sumo wrestler from a feminist?
A. A Sumo wrestler shaves his legs.

Q. What's the difference between a bandleader and a gynecologist?
A. A bandleader fucks his singers and a gynecologist sucks his fingers.

Q. Do you know what the square root of 69 is?
A. Ate something.

Q. What is the difference between "Oooh!" and "Aaah!"?
A. About three inches.

Q. What do you do in case of fallout?
A. Put it back in and take shorter strokes!

Q. Why do women have two holes so close together?
A. In case you miss.

Q. When does a Cub Scout become a Boy Scout?
A. When he eats his first Brownie

Q. How can you tell when an auto mechanic just had sex?
A. One of his fingers is clean.

Q. Why does a penis have a hole in the end?
A. So men can be open minded.

Q. What's the biggest fish in the world?
A. A hore, if you catch one you can eat her for months.

Q. How can you tell if your girlfriend wants you?
A. When you put your hand down her pants and it feels like you're feeding a horse.

Q. Have you heard about the new 'Mint flavored birth control pill for women that they take immediately before sex?
A. They're called 'Predickamints'

Q. What is the difference between a golf ball and a g-spot?
A. Men will spend two hours searching for a golf ball.

Q. What's the difference between a toad and a horny toad?
A. One goes "ribbit" the other goes "rub it".'

Q. Did you hear about the guy who finally figured out women?
A. He died laughing before he could tell anybody.

Q. What's the difference between Mad Cow disease and PMS?
A. Nothing.
Q. Why does the bride always wear white?
A. Well aren't all kitchen appliances that colour?

Q. What's the difference between parsley and pussy?
A. Nobody eats parsley.

Q. What's green, slimy and smells like Miss Piggy?
A. Kermit's Finger

Q. What do you do with 365 used rubbers?
A. Melt them down, make a tire, and call it a Goodyear.

Q. What's the difference between sin and shame?

A. It is a sin to put it in, but it's a shame to pull it out.

Q. Why did Raggedy Anne get thrown out of the toy box?
A. Because she kept sitting on Pinocchio's face moaning, "Lie to me!"

Q. Why is air a lot like sex?
A. Because it's no big deal unless you're not getting any.

Q. What did the egg say to the boiling water?
A. "How can you expect me to get hard so fast? I just got laid a minute ago."

Q. What did the potato chip say to the battery?
A. If you're Eveready, I'm Frito Lay.

Q. What's the best thing about a blow job?
A. Ten minutes of silence!

Q. What's the difference between a lesbian and a Ritz cracker?
A. Ones a snack cracker, and the others a crack snacker!

Q. What's another name for pickled bread?
A. Dill-dough

Q. Why did Frosty the Snowman pull down his pants?
A. He heard the snow blower coming.

Q: What do you call a lesbian dinosaur?
A: Lickalotopuss.

Q. What do the spice girls and a pack of M+Ms have in common?
A. There are assorted colors, but they all taste the same.

Q. What do you call an Amish guy with his hand up a horses ass?
A. A Mechanic.

Q. What do you call an Alabama farmer with a sheep under each arm?
A. Pimp.

Q. What do Eskimos get from sitting on the ice too long?

A. Polaroids.

Q. Why are women are like tires?
A. There's always a spare.
Q. What's brown and sits on a piano bench?
A. Beethoven's First Movement.

Q. What do you call a nun with a sex change operation?
A. A tran-sister.

Q. What did one gay sperm say to the other gay sperm?
A. I can't see a thing with all this shit in here!

Q. Why do women wear black underwear?
A. They are mourning for the stiff they buried the night before.

Q. How do you know when a male porn star is at the gas station?
A. Right before the gas stops pumping he pulls out the nozzle and sprays it all over the car.

Q. What is the difference between a hockey game and a High School reunion?
A. At a hockey game you see fast pucks.

Q. What do you call a vegetarian with diarrhea?
A. A salad shooter

Q. What is the difference between a bachelor and a married man?
A. Bachelor comes home, sees what's in the refrigerator, goes to bed. Married man comes home, sees what's in the bed, and goes to the refrigerator.

Q. Why did the boy fall off the swing?
A. He didn't have any arms.

Q. What's the definition of eternity?
A. The time between when you cum and she leaves.

Q. What's gray, sits at the bed and takes the piss?
A. A kidney dialysis machine.

Q. What do you call a female police officer that shaves her pubic hair?
A. Cunt Stubble.

Q. Why do only 10% of women go to heaven?
A. Because if they all went, it would be hell.

Q. What goes: "CLICK -is that it? CLICK -is that it? CLICK -is that it?"
A. A blind person with a rubix cube.

Q. Why did God invent yeast infection?
A. So women know what it feels like to live with an annoying cunt.

Q. Did you hear about the two gay guys that had an argument in the bar?
A. They went outside to exchange blows.

Q. Why did the gay guy think his lover was cheating on him?
A. He came home shit faced.

Q. What do you get when you cross a rooster with a flea?
A. An itchy cock.

Q. Why is a Laundromat a bad place for a guy to pick up women?
A. Women who can't even afford a washing machine will never be able to support you.

Q. Why are roach clips called roach clips?
A. Because "pot holder" was already taken.

Q. What's the worst part about getting a lung transplant?
A. The first couple of times you cough, its not your phlegm...

Q. Why do women have arms?
A. Have you any idea how long it would take to LICK a bathroom clean?

Q. Why is being in the military like a blowjob?

A. The closer you get to discharge, the better you feel.

Q. What's the bad news about being a test tube baby?
A. You know for sure that your dad is a wanker.

Q. How are men like noodles?
A. They're always in hot water, they lack taste, and they need dough.

Q. Why don't Canadians have group sex?
A. Too many thank-you letters to write afterwards.

Q. Why are hangovers better than women?
A. Hangovers will go away.

Q. How many honest, intelligent, caring men in the world does it take to do the dishes?
A. Both of them.

Q. What's the difference between a 'Spice Girls' video and a porn video?
A. The porn video has better music!

Q. What's the best part of having a homeless girlfriend?
A. You can drop her off where ever you want!

Q. What is the difference between Iraq's air force and the United States' Air Force?
A. The U.S. pilots break ground and fly into the wind.

Q. What is the difference between growing old and growing up?
A. Growing old is mandatory.

Q. What do you find in a clean nose?
A. Fingerprints!

Q. Did you hear about the blind circumcicionist?
A. He got the sack.

Q. Did you hear about the gay guy that's on the patch?
A. He's down to four butts a day.

Q. Did you hear about the kid napping?
A. Yeah, he woke up!

Q. Did you hear that the new and politically correct name for "lesbian".
A. It has been changed to "vagitarian".

Q. What's the definition of "Tender Love?"
A. Two gays with haemorrhoids.

Q. Did you hear about the two poofters who went to London?
A. They were REALLY pissed off when they found out Big Ben was a clock.

Q. What does a poof and an ambulance have in common?
A. They both get loaded from the rear and go whoo-whoo!

Q. How can you tell if you are in a gay amusement park?
A. They issue gerbils at the tunnel of love.

Q. Did you know 70% of the gay population were born that way?
A. The other 30% were sucked into it.

Q. Hear about the new gay sitcom?
A. "Leave it, it's Beaver."

Q. Did you hear about the gay rabbit?
A. He found a hare up his ass.

Q. How can you tell if a novel is homosexual?
A. The hero always gets his man in the end.

Q. How can you tell if a Western is homosexual?
A. All the good guys are hung.

Q. Why can't scientists find a cure for AIDS?
A. They can't get the laboratory mice to arse fuck.

Q. Why did the gay man take two aspirin with his Viagra?
A. So sex wouldn't be such a pain in the arse.

Q. Did you hear about the two gay judges?
A. They tried each other.

Q. What's the biggest crime committed by transvestites?
A. Male fraud.

Q. What's the difference between a hamster and a cow?
A. Cows survive the branding.

Q. What do a nearsighted gynaecologist and a puppy have in common?
A. A wet nose.

Q. What do you call a hillbilly who owns sheep and goats.
A. Bisexual.

Q. What's yellow and green and eats nuts?
A. Gonorrhoea.

Q. Have you heard about the new line of Tampax with bells and tinsel?
A. It's for the Christmas period.

Q. How is a pussy like a grapefruit?
A. The best ones squirt when you eat them.

Q. How can you tell she's a macho women?
A. She rolls her own tampons.

Q. Why did god give men penises?
A. So they'd always have at least one way to shut a woman up!

Q. Did you hear about the Easter egg hunt for the Alzheimer's patients?
A. They hid their own eggs!

Q. What's the hottest thing in the world?
A. Two rats fucking in a wool sock.

Q. What do your parents' car and testicles have in common?
A. Hit either one of them and you're grounded.

Q. What do you get when you cross a brassiere with Texas?
A. Playtex.

Q. What do you call a herd of cows masturbating?
A. Beef strokin' off.

Q. What's female Viagra?
A. Jewellery

Q. What do you call an anorexic prostitute?
A. Lite & Easy

Q. Why doesn't Smokey the bear have any kids?
A. Because every time his wife gets hot, he covers her with dirt and beats her with a shovel.

Q. What's the difference between the San Diego Padres and a Prostitute?
A. Nothing, they both suck!

Q. Did you hear about the new Exorcist Movie?
A. They got the Devil to come into take the Priest out of the child.

Q. How many animals can you get into a pair of tights?
A. 10 little piggies, 2 calves, 1 beaver, 1 ass, 1 pussy, thousands of hares and a dead fish no one can ever find.

Q. How can you tell if you eat pussy well?
A. You wake up in the morning with a face like a glazed doughnut and a beard like an unwashed paintbrush.

Q. Did you hear about the male prostitute who got leprosy?
A. He did okay until his business fell off.

Q. What's the best thing about marrying a woman with leprosy?
A. She can only give you lip once!

Q. If they bring shrimp home on shrimp boats, fish home on fish boats, and clams home on clam boats, what do they bring crabs home on?

A. The Captains Dinghy!

Q. What should you give a man who has everything?
A. A woman to show him how to use it.

YO MAMA

Yo mama is so fat she threw on a sheet for Halloween and went as Antarctica.

Yo mama is so ugly that just after she was born, her mother said "What a treasure!" and her father said "Yes, let's go bury it."

Yo mama so fat she's got more Chins than a Hong Kong phone book!

Yo mama is so fat that she looked up cheat codes for Wii Fit

Yo mama is so fat that the only exercise she gets is when she chases the ice cream truck.

Yo mama so old that when she was in school there was no history class

Yo mama has so many teeth missing, that it looks like her tongue is in jail.

Yo mama is like a telephone, even a 3 year old can pick her up.

Yo momma so fat she fell in love and broke it.

Yo momma so ugly even the tide won't take her out

Yo momma so stupid she stole free bread.

Yo mama so old she has a picture of Moses in her yearbook.

Yo mama so stupid that she puts lipstick on her head just to make-up her mind

Yo mama is so ugly that when she goes to the therapist, he makes her lie on the couch face down.

Yo mama so ugly her mom had to be drunk to breast feed her

Yo mama so old she knew Burger King while he was still a prince.

Yo mama is so fat that when she walked in front of the TV, I missed 3 seasons of Breaking Bad.

Yo mama is like a hockey player, she only showers after three periods.

Yo mama so stupid when your dad said it was chilly outside, she ran outside with a spoon

Yo Mama so fat when she went to the movies she sat next to everyone

Yo mama so ugly she made an onion cry.

Yo mama is so fat that I took a picture of her last Christmas and it's still printing!

Yo mama is so ugly that when she walks down the street in September, people say "Wow, is it Halloween already?"

Yo mama is so fat that when she ran away, they had to use all four sides of the milk carton to display her picture.

Yo mama is so fat that she has to put her belt on with a boomerang.

Yo mama is so ugly that that when she sits in the sand on the beach, cats try to bury her.

Yo mama so fat when she steps on a scale, it read "one at a time, please"

Yo mama is so fat that when she was diagnosed with a flesh-eating disease, the doctor gave her ten years to live.

Yo mama is so fat that at the zoo, the elephants throw HER peanuts.

Yo mama is so ugly that you have to tie a steak around her neck so the dog will play with her!

Yo mama is so fat and dumb that the only reason she opened her email was because she heard it contained spam.

Yo mama aint so bad...she would give you the hair off of her back!

Yo mama so poor your family ate cereal with a fork to save milk

Yo mama is so fat that when she asked for a waterbed, they put a blanket over the ocean!

Yo mama so poor when she goes to KFC, she has to lick other people's fingers!

Yo mama is so ugly that they push her face into dough to make gorilla cookies.

Yo mama so fat I had to take a train and two buses just to get on the her good side!

Yo mama so hairy the only language she speaks is wookie

Yo mama's glasses are so thick that when she looks on a map she can see people waving

Yo mama so old I told her to act her own age, and she died.

Yo mama is so ugly that when she looks in the mirror it says "viewer discretion is advised".

Yo mama so fat when her beeper goes off, people thought she was backing up

Yo mama house so dirty she has to wipe her feet before she goes outside.

Yo mama so fat when you get on top of her your ears pop!

Yo momma so ugly I took her to the zoo, guy at the door said "Thanks for bringing her back".

DAD JOKES

A young blonde woman is distraught because she fears her husband is having an affair, so she goes to a gun shop and buys a handgun. The next day she comes home to find her husband in bed with a beautiful redhead. She grabs the gun and holds it to her own head. The husband jumps out of bed, begging and pleading with her not to shoot herself. Hysterically the blonde responds to the husband, "Shut up...you're next!"

A woman has twins, and gives them up for adoption. One of them goes to a family in Egypt and is named 'Amal.' The other goes to a family in Spain, they name him Juan'. Years later; Juan sends a picture of himself to his mum. Upon receiving the picture, she tells her husband that she wished she also had a picture of Amal. Her husband responds, "But they are twins. If you've seen Juan, you've seen Amal."

Q: Did you hear about the flasher who was thinking of retiring?

A: He decided to stick it out for one more year.

Q: What do girls and rocks have in common?
A: Everyone skips the flat ones.

A teacher wanted to teach her students about self-esteem, so she asked anyone who thought they were stupid to stand up. One kid stood up and the teacher was surprised. She didn't think anyone would stand up so she asked him, "Why did you stand up?" He answered, "I didn't want to leave you standing up by yourself."

A child asked his father, "How were people born?" So his father said, "Adam and Eve made babies, then their babies became adults and made babies, and so on." The child then went to his mother, asked her the same question and she told him, "We were monkeys then we evolved to become like we are now." The child ran back to his father and said, "You lied to me!" His father replied, "No, your mom was talking about her side of the family."

Q: What has 100 balls and screws old ladies?
A: Bingo

Q: What do you call a smart blonde?
A: A golden retriever.

A couple is shopping in the mall for hours. The wife turns to talk to her husband and realizes he's nowhere in sight. Angry, she calls his cell phone and asks where he disappeared to. "Honey," he says, "remember that jewelery store we walked by a few years ago, and you loved the gold locket in the window but we couldn't afford it, so I told you I would buy it for you one day?" Choked up, the wife replies, "Yes, how could I forget?" Her husband goes on, "Well, I'm at the bar next door to it if you need me."

There was a blonde, a redhead, and a brunette. They were all trapped on an island and the nearest shore was 50 miles away. The redhead swam trying to make it to the other shore she swam 15 miles, drowned, and died. The brunette swam 24 miles, drowned, and died. The blonde swam 25 miles, got tired, and swam back.

Wife: "I look fat. Can you give me a compliment?"
Husband: "You have perfect eyesight."

Q: What do dolphins have that no other mammals have?
A: Baby dolphins.

An elderly woman went to her local doctor's office and asked to speak with her doctor. When the receptionist asked why she was there, she replied, I'd like to have some birth control pills. Taken back, the doctor thought for a minute and then said, "Excuse me, Mrs. Glenwood, but you're 80 years old. What would you possibly need birth control pills for?" The woman replied, "They help me sleep better." The doctor considered this for a second, and continued, "How in the world do birth control pills help you sleep?" The woman said, "I put them in my granddaughter's orange juice, and I sleep better at night."

Johnny was at school and the teacher said, "Someone use fascinate in a sentence." Sally answered, "The zoo was fascinating." The teacher said, "Sorry, Sally, I said to use fascinate in a sentence." Maria suggested, "I was fascinated at the zoo." Once again the teacher said, "No, Maria, I specifically said to use fascinate in a sentence." Johnny said, "My sister has ten buttons on her sweater." Again the teacher said, "Sorry, Johnny, I said use fascinate in a sentence." Johnny replied, "I know, but her boobs are so big she can only fasten eight."

A man buys a lie-detecting robot that slaps people who fib and tests it out at dinner. He asks his son, "Did you go to school today?" The son replies, "Yes," and the robot slaps him. The sons says, "All right, I went to the movies." The father asks, "What did you see?" and the son replies, "Toy Story 3." The robot slaps him again, and the son says, "OK, OK! It was Gang Bang 3." His father snorts and says, "When I was your age we didn't know what porn was." This time the robot slaps the father. The mother sputters in her coffee and retorts, "Ha! He's your son, after all," and the robot slaps her.

A man calls 999: "Come immediately, my little son has swallowed a condom!" After five minutes, the same man calls back and says, "Forget It, I found another one."

I was talking to a girl in the bar last night, and she said, "If you lost a few pounds, had a shave, and got your haircut, you'd look alright." I said, "If I did that, I'd be talking to your friends over there instead of you."

Two young boys walk into a pharmacy one day, pick out a box of Tampax and proceed to the checkout counter. The man at the counter asks the older boy, "Son, how old are you?" "Eight," the boy replies. The man continues, "Do you know what these are used for? "Not exactly," the boy says. "But they aren't for me. They're for my brother, he's four. We saw on TV that if you use these you would be able to swim and ride a bike. Right now he can't do either one."

A male patient is lying in bed in the hospital, wearing an oxygen mask over his mouth and nose. A young, student nurse appears to give him a partial sponge bath. "Nurse", he mumbled from behind the mask, "are my testicles black?" Embarrassed, the young nurse replies, "I don't know, sir. I'm only here to wash your upper body and feet." He struggles to ask again, "nurse, are my testicles black?" Concerned, she overcomes her embarrassment and sheepishly pulls back the covers. She raises his gown, holds his manhood in one hand and his testicles in the otherShe looks very closely and says, "don't worry, sir. They look fine." The man pulls off his oxygen mask, smiles at her and says very slowly, "thank you very much. That was wonderful, but, listen very, very closely: are my test results back?"

An old, blind cowboy wanders into an all-girl biker bar by mistake. After sitting there for a while, he yells to the bartender, 'Hey, you wanna hear a blonde joke?' The bar immediately falls absolutely silent. In a very deep, husky voice, the woman next to him says, "Before you tell that joke, Cowboy, I think it is only fair,

Given that you are blind, that you should know five things: 1. The bartender is a blonde girl with a baseball bat. 2. The bouncer is a blonde girl. 3. I'm a 6-foot tall, 175-pound blonde woman with a black belt in karate. 4. The woman sitting next to me is blonde and a professional weight lifter. 5. The lady to your right is blonde and a professional wrestler. Now, think about it seriously, Cowboy. Do you still wanna tell that blonde joke?"
The blind cowboy thinks for a second, shakes his head and mutters, 'No...not if I'm gonna have to explain it five times."

What did one saggy boob say to the other saggy boob? "We better get some support before someone thinks we're nuts!"

Two girls are drinking at a bar. One says, "If I have another drink, I'm going to feel it."
The friend replies, "If I have another, I don't care who feels it."

Just read that 4,153,237 people got married last year, not to cause any trouble but shouldn't that be an even number?

I think my neighbor is stalking me as she's been googling my name on her computer. I saw it through my telescope last night.

My dad died when we couldn't remember his blood type. As he died, he kept insisting for us to "be positive," but it's hard without him.

Today a man knocked on my door and asked for a small donation towards the local swimming pool. I gave him a glass of water.

I hate people who use big words just to make themselves look perspicacious.

I asked my wife what she wanted for Christmas. She told me "Nothing would make her happier than a diamond necklace" So I bought her nothing.

Turning vegan is a big missed steak.

Hospitality: making your guests feel like they're at home, even if you wish they were.

I saw an ad for burial plots, and thought to myself this is the last thing I need.

I just found out I'm colorblind. The diagnosis came completely out of the purple.

The average woman would rather have beauty than brains, because the average man can see better than he can think.

The reward for a job well done is more work.

A conclusion is the part where you got tired of thinking.

I was going to look for my missing watch, but I could never find the time.

Money isn't everything but it sure keeps you in touch with your children.

Atheism is a non-prophet organization.

I used to think I was indecisive, but now I'm not too sure.

Dating a single mother is like continuing from somebody else's saved game.

My job is secure. No one else wants it.

A clean house is the sign of a broken computer.

Claustrophobic people are more productive thinking out of the box.

I saw a guy on his motorcycle and the back of his shirt said "If you can read this the b*tch fell off."

I hate jokes about prom. The punch line is always too long.

I changed my password to "incorrect". So whenever I forget what it is the computer will say "Your password is incorrect".

How many more times are my kids going to ask me if I know where something is before they realize they're asking the wrong parent?

Better to understand a little than to misunderstand a lot.

A good wife always forgives her husband when she's wrong.

I find it ironic that the colors red, white, and blue stand for freedom until they are flashing behind you.

eBay is so useless. I tried to look up lighters and all they had was 13,749 matches

A couple years ago my therapist told me I had problems letting go of the past.

Never laugh at your girlfriends choices... your one of them.

Some of us learn from the mistakes of others; the rest of us have to be the others.

The best time to start thinking about your retirement is before the boss does.

I used to be in a band, we were called 'lost dog'. You probably saw our posters.

I am not a vegetarian because I love animals. I am a vegetarian because I hate plants.

The reason grandchildren and grandparents get along so well is because they have a common "enemy".

I have as much authority as the Pope, i just don't have as many people who believe it.

My parents won't say which of their six kids they love the best, but they have told me I finished just out of the top five.

I would like to thank everybody that stuck by my side for those five long minutes my house didn't have internet.

Never test the depth of the water with both feet.

A TV can insult your intelligence, but nothing rubs it in like a computer.

Let me make this simple, I want to be invited but I don't want to go.

Diet Day #1 - I removed all the fattening food from my house. It was delicious.

Team work is important; it helps to put the blame on someone else.

My kids are very optimistic. Every glass they leave sitting around the house is at least half full.

Why should blondes not be given coffee breaks? It takes too long to retrain them.

Wise people think all they say, fools say all they think.

I saw two guys wearing matching clothing and I asked if they were gay. They quickly arrested me.

With great reflexes comes great response ability.

Absolutely furious that a handful of things not suited to my taste are well liked by others.

I live in constant fear that my kid will become a famous artist or painter and I will have thrown out about a trillion dollars of her work.

Two antennas met on a roof, fell in love and got married. The ceremony wasn't much, but the reception was excellent.

When I found out that my toaster wasn't waterproof, I was shocked.

Time is what keeps things from happening all at once.

Never get into fights with ugly people, they have nothing to lose.

For maximum attention, nothing beats a good mistake.

Isn't it great to live in the 21st century? Where deleting history has become more important than making it.

My girlfriend said, "You act like a detective too much. I want to split up." "Good idea," I replied. "We can cover more ground that way."

Life is all about perspective. The sinking of the Titanic was a miracle to the lobsters in the ship's kitchen.

My wife told me to stop impersonating a flamingo. I had to put my foot down.

I wanna hang a map of the world in my house. Then I'm gonna put pins into all the locations that I've traveled to. But first, I'm gonna have to travel to the top two corners of the map so it won't fall down.

To the mathematicians who thought of the idea of zero, thanks for nothing!

I'm sorry I wasn't part of your past, can I make it up by being in your future?

Somewhere an elderly lady reads a book on how to use the internet, while a young boy googles "how to read a book".

My mind's made up, don't confuse me with facts.

I would give my dad what he really wants on Father's Day, but I can't afford to move out yet.

Retirement is wonderful. It's doing nothing without worrying about getting caught at it.

It's better to let someone think you are an Idiot than to open your mouth and prove it.

If we aren't supposed to eat animals, why are they made with meat?

If at first you don't succeed, we have a lot in common.

Before having a kid the most important thing to ask yourself is "Am I ready to watch the exact same cartoon on repeat for the next 4 years?"

When I call a family meeting I turn off the house wifi and wait for them all to come running.

R.I.P boiled water. You will be mist.

The trouble with doing something right the first time is that nobody appreciates how difficult it was.

Whenever someone calls me ugly, I get super sad and hug them, because I know how tough life is for the visually impaired.

Don't be irreplaceable - if you cannot be replaced, you cannot be promoted.

I'm great at multitasking. I can waste time, be unproductive, and procrastinate all at once.

Another World's Oldest Man has died. This is beginning to look suspicious.

How do people lose their kids at the supermarket? Seriously, any tips would be greatly appreciated.

It's not peer pressure, it's just your turn.

Beauty is only skin deep ...but ugly goes all the way to the bone!

You have two parts of brain, 'left' and 'right'. In the left side, there's nothing right. In the right side, there's nothing left.

I was such an ugly kid. When I played in the sandbox the cat kept covering me up.

90% of women don't like men in pink shirts. Ironically, 90% of men in pink shirts don't like women.

For Valentines Day I have been contemplating my current and past relationships. I organized the data and plotted it using an Ex-Axis and a Why-Axis.

Just asked my wife what she's "burning up for dinner" and it turned out to be all of my personal belongings.

Childs experience: if a mother is laughing at the fathers jokes, it means they have guests.

Is your ass jealous of the amount of shit that just came out of your mouth?

A woman never wakes up her second baby just to see it smile.

What is the best thing about living in Switzerland? Well, the flag is a big plus.

The only reason the term 'Ladies first' was invented was for the guy to check out the woman's ass.

Why can't women read maps? Only the male mind can comprehend the concept of one inch equaling a mile.

I eat my tacos over a Tortilla. That way when stuff falls out, BOOM, another taco.

There is no dance without the dancers.

Money talks ...but all mine ever says is good-bye.

My wife and I were happy for twenty years. Then we met.

My five-year-old: "I don't want to be your daughter anymore. I QUIT!" No two-week notice or anything. She'd better not expect a reference.

Q: What do you call the security outside of a Samsung Store? A: Guardians of the Galaxy.

I wonder what my parents did to fight boredom before the internet. I asked my 17 brothers and sisters and they didn't know either.

If a guy remembers the color of your eyes after the first date, chances are... you have small boobs.

It is true that you may fool all of the people some of the time; you can even fool some the people all of the time; but you can't fool all of the people all of the time.

Why are there so many old people in Church? They're cramming for the final.

Clinging on to past and living is like driving forward while watching the rear view mirror...

My wife is so negative. I remembered the car seat, the stroller, AND the diaper bag. Yet all she can talk about is how I forgot the baby.

If a short psychic broke out of jail, then you'd have a small medium at large.

A clean desk is a sign of a cluttered desk drawer.

A wise man once said... Nothing, he only listened.

Is google a woman? Because it won't let you finish your sentence without coming up with other suggestions.

Strong people don't put others down. They lift them up and slam them on the ground for maximum damage.

A man is being arrested by a female police officer, who informs him, "Anything you say can and will be held against you." The man replies, "Boobs!"

Why do mother kangaroos hate rainy days? Because their kids have to play inside!

If a person told you they were a pathological liar, should you believe them?

My dog used to chase people on a bike a lot. It got so bad, finally I had to take his bike away.

You're old enough to remember when emojis were called "hieroglyphics."

I saw six men kicking and punching the mother-in-law. My neighbour said 'Are you going to help?' I said 'No, six should be enough.'

If you think nobody cares whether you're alive, try missing a couple of payments.

My doctor advised me to kill people. Not in such words of course, he just said that I must diminish the amount of stress in my life.

Live every day like it was the last day, and one day you won't miss.

Men approve of premarital sex until daughters are born.

Do not argue with an idiot. He will drag you down to his level and beat you with experience.

I don't engage in mental combat with the unarmed.

My wife's not too smart. I told her, our kids were spoiled. She said, "All kids smell that way."

Middle age is when you're faced with two temptations and you choose the one that will get you home by nine o'clock.

Whatever you do always give 100 %. Unless you are donating blood.

Oxygen is proven to be a toxic gas. Anyone who inhales oxygen will normally dies within 80 years.

Did you hear about the kidnapping at school?
It's okay. He woke up.

My doctor told me that jogging could add years to my life. He was right—I feel ten years older already.

If Bill Gates had a penny for every time I had to reboot my computer ...oh wait, he does.

I ordered 2000 lbs. of chinese soup. It was Won Ton.

Nostalgia isn't what it used to be.

I used to be addicted to soap, but I'm clean now.

Relationships are a lot like algebra. Have you ever looked at your X and wondered Y?

I love the F5 key. It ´s just so refreshing.

There is a new trend in our office; everyone is putting names on their food. I saw it today, while I was eating a sandwich named Kevin.

My boss says I intimidate the other employees, so I just stared at him until he apologized.

He is so old that he gets nostalgic when he sees the Neolithic cave paintings.

Archeologist: someone whose carreer lies in ruins.

After kissing a girl on her sofa she said "let's take this upstairs"."Ok" I said "You grab one end and I'll grab the other"

I can't believe I got fired from the calendar factory. All I did was take a day off.

I'm reading a book about anti-gravity. It's impossible to put down.

Support bacteria - they're the only culture some people have.

I'm reading a horror story in Braille. Something bad is about to happen... I can feel it.

I got caught in police speed trap yesterday. The officer walked up to my car and said "I've been waiting all day for you " Well I said. I got here as fast as I could.

Why do the French eat snails? They don't like fast food.

I wasn't originally going to get a brain transplant, but then I changed my mind.

I always wanted to be somebody, but now I realize I should have been more specific.

Experience is what you get when you didn't get what you wanted.

There are three kinds of people: Those who can count and those who can't.

Did you hear about the guy who got hit in the head with a can of soda? He was lucky it was a soft drink.

A teacher asks a student, "Are you ignorant or just apathetic?" The kid answers, "I don't know and I don't care."

I saw my dad chopping up onions today and I cried. Onions was a good dog.

Don't spell part backwards. It's a trap.

Last Father's Day my son gave me something I always wanted: the keys to my car.

It must be difficult to post inspirational Tweets when your blood type is B Negative.

I gave up my seat to a blind person in the bus. That is how I lost my job as a bus driver.

A courtroom artist was arrested today for an unknown reason... details are sketchy.

Apparently I snore so loudly that it scares everyone in the car I'm driving.

I want to die peacefully in my sleep, like my grandfather.. Not screaming and yelling like the passengers in his car.

I'm really good at stuff until people watch me do that stuff.

A dad is washing the car with his son. After a moment, the son asks his father, "Do you think we could use a sponge instead?"

It's ok computer, I go to sleep after 20 minutes of inactivity too.

Two wrongs don't make a right, take your parents as an example.

Children in the back seats of cars cause accidents, but accidents in the back seats of cars cause children.

How long have I been working for this company? Ever since they threatened to fire me.

Parenting is filled with wonder. Like wondering why your 4 years old raced into the kitchen and quietly grabbed a handful of napkins.

I named my hard drive "dat ass" so once a month my computer asks if I want to 'back dat ass up'.

Laugh and the world laughs with you. Snore and you sleep alone

The severity of the itch is inversely proportional to the ability to reach it.

When someone asks me if I'm seeing anyone, I automatically assume they're talking about a psychiatrist.

If you can't remember my name, just say 'donuts'. I'll turn around and look.

Two blondes were driving to Disneyland. The sign said, "Disneyland Left". So they started crying and went home.

Doesn't expecting the unexpected make the unexpected become the expected?

Sometimes the first step to forgiveness, is realising the other person was born an idiot.

"No, thanks. I'm a vegetarian." is a fun thing to say when someone hands you their baby.

Eat right. Stay fit. Die anyway.

If a woman sleeps with 10 men she's a slut, but if a man does it... He's gay, definitely gay.

How do you know your old? People call at 9 p.m. and ask, "Did I wake you?"

I've been taking Viagra for my sunburn. It doesn't cure it but it keeps the sheets off my legs at night.

I'd tell you a chemistry joke but I know I wouldn't get a reaction.

Chinese kid was born before the due date. Parents named him Sudden Lee.

Why does it feel like time slows down during the day when you're at work and rapidly speeds up at night when you get home?

Women might be able to fake orgasms. But men can fake a whole relationship.

Isn't it weird how when a cop drives by you feel paranoid instead of protected.

My dad sent me to a psychiatrist for wearing his bra again.

The worst part about working for the department of unemployment is when you get fired you still have to show up the next day.

I found a rock yesterday which measured 1760 yards in length. Must be some kind of milestone.

If 4 out of 5 people SUFFER from diarrhea... does that mean that one enjoys it?

Life is like toilet paper, you're either on a roll or taking shit from some asshole.

Work is for people who don't know how to fish.

My speech today will be like a mini-skirt. Long enough to cover the essentials but short enough to hold your attention!

A girl phoned me the other day and said, "Come on over, there's nobody home." I went over. Nobody was home.

Anger; the feeling that makes your mouth work faster than your mind.

If you can smile when things go wrong, you have someone in mind to blame.

What's worse than waking up at a party and finding a penis drawn on your face? Finding out it was traced.

A study of economics usually reveals that the best time to buy anything was last year.

Your family tree must be a cactus because everybody on it is a prick.

My girlfriends dad asked me what I do. Apparently, "your daughter" wasn't the right answer.

If you see me smiling it's because I'm thinking of doing something evil or naughty. If you see me laughing it's because I've already done it.

It's always a good idea to make friends with babies. That's free cake once a year for a lifetime.

A straight face and a sincere-sounding "Huh?" have gotten me out of more trouble than I can remember.

Get a new car for your spouse - it'll be a great trade!

I tried to catch some fog, I mist.

Always remember you're unique, just like everyone else.

I have a few jokes about unemployed people but it doesn't matter none of them work.

They used to time me with a stopwatch... now they use a calendar.

I hate Russian dolls, they're so full of themselves.

I think men who have a pierced ear are better prepared for marriage. They've experienced pain and bought jewelry.

A fine is a tax for doing wrong. A tax is a fine for doing well.

Subway is definitely the healthiest fast food available because they make you get out of the car.

The last thing I want to do is hurt you. But it's still on the list.

Depression: A period during which we have to get along without the things our grandparents never dreamed of.

Why do I keep paying the bills? It just encourages them to send more.

Don't worry guys, my wife just turned the car radio down so we shouldn't be lost much longer.

I'm the kind of guy who stops the microwave at 1 second just to feel like a bomb disposal expert.

The hardness of butter is directly proportional to the softness of the bread.

A good time to keep your mouth shut is when you're in deep water.

Your birth certificate is an apology letter from the condom factory.

I'm glad I know sign language, it's pretty handy.

Did you hear about the man who jumped off a bridge in France? He was in Sein.

I'm at the age where I have to make a noise when I bend over. It's the law.

It's been raining for 3 days without stopping. My wife is in depression, she is standing and looking through the window. If the rain doesn't stop tomorrow, I'll have to let her in.

I think it's wrong that only one company makes the game Monopoly.

Got an e-mail today from a "bored housewife 33, looking for some action!" I've sent her my ironing, that'll keep her busy.

Middle age is when work is a lot less fun and fun a lot more work.

Wouldn't exercise be more fun if calories screamed while you burned them?

Up until I bought this bag of crisps I thought the air was free.

When I was young, I always felt like a male trapped in a females body. Then I was born

Did you hear about these new reversible jackets? I'm excited to see how they turn out.

Thieves had broken into my house and stolen everything except my soap, shower gel, towels and deodorant. Dirty Bastards.

I remember being in so much debt that I couldn't afford my electricity bills, it was a dark time.

I sleep better naked ... why can't the flight attendant understand this?

My nephew found a cassette tape in my house. It was like watching early man discover fire.

It's bad luck to be superstitious.

What do you call a cow during an earthquake? A milkshake.

Circumcision is popular because Jewish girls won't touch anything that's not at least 15% off.

You're not fat, you're just... easier to see.

A woman gets on a bus with her baby. The bus driver says: "Ugh, that's the ugliest baby I've ever seen!" The woman walks to the rear of the bus and sits down, fuming. She says to a man next to her: "The driver just insulted me!" The man says: "You go up there and tell him off. Go on, I'll hold your monkey for you."

I went to the zoo the other day, there was only one dog in it, it was a shitzu."

Dyslexic man walks into a bra"

A young blonde woman is distraught because she fears her husband is having an affair, so she goes to a gun shop and buys a handgun. The next day she comes home to find her husband in bed with a beautiful redhead. She grabs the gun and holds it to her own head. The husband jumps out of bed, begging and pleading with her not to shoot herself. Hysterically the blonde responds to the husband, "Shut up...you're next!"

Police arrested two kids yesterday, one was drinking battery acid, the other was eating fireworks. They charged one - and let the other one off.

Another one was: Doc, I can't stop singing the 'Green Green Grass of Home'. He said: 'That sounds like Tom Jones syndrome'. 'Is it common?'I asked. 'It's not unusual' he replied.

I'm on a whiskey diet. I've lost three days already.

A man walks into a bar with a roll of tarmac under his arm and says: "Pint please, and one for the road."

My mother-in-law fell down a wishing well, I was amazed, I never knew they worked.

I saw this bloke chatting up a cheetah; I thought, "He's trying to pull a fast one".

A woman has twins, and gives them up for adoption. One of them goes to a family in Egypt and is named 'Emol.' The other goes to a family in Spain, they name him 'Juan'. Years later; Juan sends a picture of himself to his mum. Upon receiving the picture, she tells her husband that she wished she also had a picture of emol. Her husband responds, "But they are twins. If you've seen Juan, you've seen Emol."

I went to buy some camouflage trousers the other day but I couldn't find any.

My therapist says I have a preoccupation with vengeance. We'll see about that."

I rang up British Telecom, I said, "I want to report a nuisance caller", he said "Not you again".

I met a Dutch girl with inflatable shoes last week, phoned her up to arrange a date but unfortunately she'd popped her clogs.

A jump-lead walks into a bar. The barman says "I'll serve you, but don't start anything"

Slept like a log last night........ Woke up in the fireplace.

Went to the paper shop - but it had blown away.

A group of chess enthusiasts checked into a hotel and were standing in the lobby discussing their recent tournament victories. After about an hour, the manager came out of the office and asked them to disperse. "But why?" they asked, as they moved off. "because," he said "I can't stand chess nuts boasting in an open foyer."

I was in Tesco's and I saw this man and woman wrapped in a barcode. I said, "Are you two an item?"

I'm in great mood tonight because the other day I entered a competition and I won a years supply of Marmite......... one jar.

There was a man who entered a local paper's pun contest.. He sent in ten different puns, in the hope that at least one of the puns would win. Unfortunately, no pun in ten did.

I backed a horse last week at ten to one. It came in at quarter past four.

I swear, the other day I bought a packet of peanuts, and on the packet it said "may contain nuts." Well, YES! That's what I bought the buggers for! You'd be annoyed if you opened it and a socket set fell out!"

A lorry-load of tortoises crashed into a trainload of terrapins, What a turtle disaster

My phone will ring at 2 in the morning, and my wife'll look at me and go, "Who's that calling at this time?' "I don't know! If I knew that we wouldn't need the bloody phone!"

Two Eskimos sitting in a kayak were chilly. But when they lit a fire in the craft, it sank, proving once and for all that you can't have your kayak and heat it.

I'll tell you what I love doing more than anything: trying to pack myself in a small suitcase. I can hardly contain myself.

So I met this gangster who pulls up the back of people's pants, it was Wedgie Kray.

ONE LINERS

Went to the corner shop - bought 4 corners.

A seal walks into a club...

42.7 percent of all statistics are made up on the spot.

99 percent of lawyers give the rest a bad name.

A bartender is just a pharmacist with a limited inventory.

A clear conscience is usually the sign of a bad memory.

A closed mouth gathers no foot.

A day without sunshine is like, night.

A diplomat is someone who can tell you to go to hell in such a way that you will look forward to the trip.

A flashlight is a case for holding dead batteries.

All generalisations are false, including this one.

Always try to be modest and be proud of it!

Anything worth taking seriously is worth making fun of.

Artificial Intelligence usually beats real stupidity.

Assassins do it from behind.

Beauty is in the eye of the beer holder.

Beer: It's not just for breakfast anymore.

Better to understand a little than to misunderstand a lot.

Bills travel through the mail at twice the speed of cheques
Borrow money from a pessimist, they don't expect it back.

Boycott shampoo! Demand the REAL poo!

Chocolate: the OTHER major food group.

Consciousness: That annoying time between naps.

Death is hereditary.

Despite the cost of living, have you noticed how popular it remains?

Diplomacy is the art of saying good doggie while looking for a bigger stick.

Do not walk behind me, for I may not lead. Do not walk ahead of me, for I may not follow. Do not walk beside me, either. Just leave me alone.

Don't be irreplaceable; if you can't be replaced, you can't be promoted.

Don't drink and drive. You might hit a bump and spill your drink.

Don't piss me off! I'm running out of places to hide the bodies.

Don't take life too seriously, you won't get out alive.

Duct tape is like the force, it has a light side and a dark side and it holds the universe together.

Eagles may soar, but weasels don't get sucked into jet engines.

Energizer Bunny arrested and charged with battery.

Ever notice how fast Windows runs? Neither did I.

Ever stop to think, and forget to start again?

Everyone has a photographic memory. Some don't have film.

Experience is something you don't get until just after you need it.

Experience is what you get when you didn't get what you wanted.

Few women admit their age. Few men act theirs.

For every action, there is an equal and opposite criticism.

For Sale: Parachute. Only used once, never opened, small stain.

Friends help you move. Real friends help you move bodies.

Friends may come and go, but enemies tend to accumulate.

Generally speaking, you aren't learning much when your mouth is moving.

Genius does what it must, talent does what it can, and you had best do what you're told.

Give a man a fish and he will eat for a day. Teach him how to fish, and he will sit in a boat and drink beer all day.

Give me ambiguity or give me something else.

Good judgment comes from bad experience and a lot of that comes from bad judgment.

Hard work has a future payoff. Laziness pays off now.

He who laughs last thinks slowest.

Honk if you love peace and quiet.

Honk if you want to see my finger.

How do you tell when you run out of invisible ink?

How does Teflon stick to the pan?

I couldn't repair your brakes, so I made your horn louder.

I don't suffer from insanity. I enjoy every minute of it.

I get enough exercise just pushing my luck.

I just got lost in thought. It was unfamiliar territory.

I need someone really bad. Are you really bad?

I poured Spot remover on my dog. Now he's gone.

I tried sniffing Coke once, but the ice cubes got stuck in my nose.

I used to be indecisive. Now I'm not sure.

I used to have a handle on life, and then it broke.

I used to have an open mind but my brains kept falling out.

I won't rise to the occasion, but I'll slide over to it.

I wouldn't be caught dead with a necrophiliac.

I'm as confused as a baby in a topless bar.

I'm not a complete idiot, some parts are missing!

I'm writing a book. I've got the page numbers done.

If at first, you don't succeed, destroy all evidence that you tried.

If at first, you don't succeed, skydiving is not for you.

If you can't convince them, confuse them.

If you tell the truth you don't have to remember anything.

It IS as bad as you think, and they ARE out to get you.

It is far more impressive when others discover your good qualities without your help.

It may be that your sole purpose in life is simply to serve as a warning to others.

It's always darkest before dawn. So if you're going to steal the neighbour's newspaper, that's the time to do it.

It's lonely at the top, but you eat better.

Join the Army, meet interesting people, and kill them.

Love may be blind but marriage is a real eye-opener.

Make it idiot proof and someone will make a better idiot.

Monday is an awful way to spend 1/7th of your life.

Multitasking means screwing up several things at once.

Never do card tricks for the group you play poker with.

Never mess up an apology with an excuse.

Never miss a good chance to shut up.

Never underestimate the power of stupid people in large groups.

Oh Lord, give me patience, and GIVE IT TO ME NOW!

On the other hand, you have different fingers.

Plan to be spontaneous, tomorrow.

Pride is what we have. Vanity is what others have.

Puritanism: The haunting fear that someone somewhere may be happy.

Quantum mechanics: The dreams stuff is made of.

Quickly, I must hurry, for there go my people and I am their leader.

Reality is a crutch for people who can't handle drugs.

Remember half the people you know are below average.

Save the whales. Collect the whole set

Save your breath. You'll need it to blow up your date!

Sex is like air; it's not important unless you aren't getting any.

Shin: a device for finding furniture in the dark.

Smile, it's the second best thing you can do with your lips.

Some days you are the bug, some days you are the windscreen.

Some drink at the fountain of knowledge. Others just gargle.

Some people are only alive because it is illegal to shoot them.

Success always occurs in private and failure in full view.

Suicidal twin kills sister by mistake!

Support bacteria, they're the only culture some people have.

The colder the x-ray table, the more of your body is required on it.

The early bird may get the worm, but the second mouse gets the cheese.

The journey of a thousand miles begins with a broken fan belt and a flat tire.

The more you complain, the longer God makes you live.

The only substitute for good manners is fast reflexes.

The problem with the gene pool is that there is no lifeguard.

The quickest way to double your money is to fold it in half and put it back in your pocket.

The severity of the itch is inversely proportional to the ability to reach it.

The sex was so good that even the neighbours had a cigarette.

The shortest distance between two points is under construction.

The sooner you fall behind the more time you'll have to catch up.

There are two theories to arguing with women. Neither one works.

Things are more like they are now than they ever were before.

To succeed in politics, it is often necessary to rise above your principles.

Wanted: Meaningful overnight relationship.

Warning: Dates in calendar are closer than they appear.

We have enough youth, how about a fountain of smart?

We were born naked, wet and hungry. Then things got worse.

Wear short sleeves! Support your right to bare arms!

What happens if you get scared half to death twice?

What is a free gift? Aren't all gifts free?

What's the speed of dark?

When everything's coming your way, you're in the wrong lane and going the wrong way.

When there's a will, I want to be in it.

When you don't know what you are doing, do it neatly.

Why do psychics have to ask you for your name?

Why is abbreviation such a long word?

Why isn't phonetic spelt the way it sounds?

Women who seek to be equal to men lack ambition.

You are depriving some poor village of its idiot.

You have the right to remain silent. Anything you say will be misquoted then used against you.

You're just jealous because the voices are talking to me and not you!

Your gene pool could use a little chlorine.

Your kid may be an honours student, but you're still an idiot.

Never interrupt your opponent while he's making a mistake.

Sarcasm helps keep people from understanding you're saying what you really think of them.

I once prayed to God for a bike, but quickly found out He didn't work that way—so I stole a bike and prayed for His forgiveness.

A train station is where the train stops. A bus station is where the bus stops. On my desk, I have a work station...

You can't be late until you show up.

War doesn't determine who's right—it determines who's left.

If you think things can't get worse, it's probably only because you lack sufficient imagination.

Parents spend the first part of our lives teaching us to walk and talk and the rest of it telling us to sit down and shut up.

Expecting the world to treat you fairly because you are good is like expecting the bull not to charge because you are a vegetarian.

Books have knowledge, knowledge is power, power corrupts, corruption is a crime, and crime doesn't pay. So if you keep reading, you'll go broke.

You can go anywhere you want if you look serious and carry a clipboard.

It may look like I'm doing nothing, but I'm actively waiting for my problems to go away.

Every rule has an exception, especially this one.

Don't let your mind wander—it's too little to be let out alone.

I'd call you a tool, but even they serve a purpose.

Death is life's way of telling you that you've been fired. Suicide is your way to tell life, "You can't fire me, I quit!"

Never argue with idiots. They drag you down to their level, then beat you with experience.

I wouldn't say you're stupid. You are, but I wouldn't say it.

If at first you don't succeed, destroy any evidence that you ever tried.

If at first you don't succeed, redefine success.

If you can't beat them, arrange to have them beaten.

Why does life keep teaching me lessons I have no desire to learn?

I have a busy day ahead: I have trouble to start, rumors to spread, and people to argue with.

I am a bomb technician. If you see me running, try to keep up.

Learn from Pandora's mistake—think outside the box.

I wonder if Ikea has a decaf coffee table.

If a mute person burps, does it make a sound?

I was complimented on my driving today. Someone left a note on my windshield that said, "Parking Fine."

Finding a job in this economy is like playing Where's Waldo?—except that Waldo is looking for a job, too.

Today, I saw a commercial for the Snuggie. I thought it was stupid idea, but I couldn't change the channel because I was under a blanket and didn't want my arms to get cold reaching for the remote.

Words can only hurt you if you try to read them. Don't play their game.

I feel like getting something done today, so I'm just going to sit here until that feeling passes...

I hear there is scientific proof that birthdays are good for you: the more you have, the longer you live.

Tip of the week: When going through airport customs and the TSA agent asks, "Do you have any firearms with you?" do not reply, "What do you need?"

I no longer question authority, I annoy authority. More effect, less effort.

I just read a list titled "100 Things to Do Before You Die." I'm pretty surprised "yell for help" wasn't one of them.

I went to the book store earlier to buy the book Where's Waldo. When I got there, I couldn't find the book anywhere. Well played, Waldo, well played.

It recently became apparent to me that the letters "T" and "G" are far too close together on a keyboard. This is why I'll never be ending an e-mail with the phrase "Regards" ever again.

I have an oven with a "stop time" button. It's probably meant to be "stop timer," but I don't touch it, just in case.

When a fly or small bug lands on your computer screen, has your first reaction ever been to try and scare it with the cursor?

People think I'm too patronizing (that means I treat them as if they're stupid).

The fact that I woke up this morning means that the assassins have failed again.

If your relationship status says, "It's complicated," maybe you should stop kidding yourself and change it to "Single."

I dream of a better world, where chickens can cross the road without anyone questioning their motives.

How long do you think it would take to solve a Rubik's cube if you were color blind?

I used to be good at sports. Then I realized that I could buy trophies. Now I'm good at everything.

I decided to cancel my Twitter account. I don't want to sound paranoid, but I was pretty sure people were following me.
"Dammit I'm mad" is spelled the same way backwards. Think about it.

If you find it hard to laugh at yourself, I would be happy to do it for you.

Who is Pete and why is it for his sake?

MORE DAD JOKES

A bloke is showing two young American girls around London and they come to a Pelican crossing. He presses the button and the pedestrian signal goes 'bleep-bleep-bleep-bleep....' 'Whats that for?' asked one of the girls. 'Oh thats just to let the blind know that the lights have changed' said the bloke. 'My Gaad' she said, really shocked, 'in the States we don't even let them drive...'

How do you know when a cabbage is boiled?? The wheelchair floats to the top

Three disabled guys (a blind man, an amputee, and a guy in a wheelchair) are flying back with the USA team from the Paralympic games in the Middle East when their plane crashes in the Sahara Desert. The three disabled guys (the only survivors) are now stranded and wait for someone to rescue them, but no one showed. They start to get real thirsty, so they decide to seek out water.
The amputee leads the way, with the blind man pushing the guy in the wheelchair; and, eventually they find an oasis. The amputee leader goes into the water first, cools himself down, drinks a load of water, walks out the other side and lo and behold, he has a NEW LEG! He gets excited and encourages his friends to do the same. The blind man offers to push the guy in the wheelchair,
but he gets refused because the guy in the chair wants to be Mr Independent and isists the blind man goes ahead first. So he goes into the water, cools himself down, drinks a load of water, walks out the other side and lo and behold, he can SEE! Now the guy in

the wheelchair's getting really excited, starts pushing with all his might, goes into the water, cools himself down, drinks
a load of water, and wheels out the other side. Lo and behold, NEW TIRES!!!

There once was a lady who was tired of living alone. So she put an ad in the paper which outlined her requirements. She wanted a man who 1) would treat her nicely, 2) wouldn't run away from her, and 3) would be good in bed.
Then, one day, she heard the doorbell ring. She answered it, and there on the front porch was a man in a wheel chair who didn't have any arms or legs.
"I'm here about the ad you put in the paper. As you can see, I have no arms so I can't beat you, and I have no legs so I can't run away from you."
"Yes, but are you good in bed?"
"How do you think I rang the doorbell?"

There was a man who got into a car accident.
He was soon rushed to the hospital. The left side of his body was completely paralyzed.
The doctor said, "He was going to be all right."

Three blokes enter a disabled swimming contest.
The first has no arms the second no legs and the third has no body, just a head.
They all line up, the whistle blows and "splash" they're all in the pool. The guy with no arms takes the lead instantly, but the guy with no legs is closing fast. The head sank straight to the bottom. Ten lengths later and the guy with no legs finishes first.
He can still see bubbles coming from the bottom of the pool, so he decides he had better dive down to rescue the head guy. He picks up the head, swims back up to the surface and places the head at the side of the pool, where-upon the head starts coughing and spluttering.
Eventually the head catches his breath and shouts: "Three god-

damn years I've spent learning to swim with my goddamn ears, then five seconds before the whistle, some bastard puts a swimming cap on me"

One day, three boys were walking over a bridge when they heard a guy yelling for help.

It was President Trump. He was drowning, and the three boys rescued him.

He thanked them dearly and promised them whatever they wanted as a reward.

The first boy wanted $10,000, so Trump gave him the money.

The second boy wanted a Ferrari, so Trump gave the boy a Ferrari.

The third boy wanted a wheelchair , Trump said, "Why do you want one of those, son, you're not disabled ."

The boy replied,"I will be when my dad finds out whose life I just saved."

April and I were lying in bed the other day. My hands were slowly finding their way across her body. I whispered, "I'm gonna make you the happiest woman in the world." She whispered back, "I'll miss you."

My wife dresses to kill. She also cooks the same way.

I bought my wife a new car. She called and said, "There was water in the carburetor."

I asked her , "Where's the car?" She replied, "In the lake."

Never go to bed mad. Stay up and fight.

When a man steals your wife, there is no better revenge than to let him keep her.

I haven't spoken to my wife in 18 months - I don't like to interrupt her.

My girlfriend told me I should be more affectionate. So I got myself two girlfriends.

Young Son: Is it true, Dad, that in some parts of Africa a man doesn't know his wife until he marries her?
Dad: That happens in every country, son.

There was a man who said, "I never knew what real happiness was until I got married; then it was too late.

A man placed an ad in the classifieds: "Wife wanted."
The next day he received a hundred letters.
They all said the same : "You can have mine."

A woman was telling her friend, "I made my husband a millionaire."
"And what was he before you married him?" asked the friend.
"A billionaire." she replied,

The trouble with being the best man at a wedding is that you never get to prove it.

A man, upon his engagement, went to his father and said," Dad! I've found a woman just like mother"
His father replied, "So what do you want? sympathy?"

Eighty percent of married men cheat in America. The rest cheat in Europe.

Marriage is the triumph of imagination over intelligence.
Second marriage is the triumph of hope over experience.

If you want your spouse to listen and pay strict attention to every word you say, talk in your sleep.

It's not true that married men live longer than single men. It only seems longer.

Losing a wife can be very hard. In my case, it was almost impossible.

A man was complaining to a friend: "I had it all - money, a beautiful house, a big car, the love of a beautiful woman - and then,

BAM!, it was all gone!"
"What happened?" asked his friend. "My wife found out..."

Just think, if it weren't for marriage, men would go through life thinking they had no faults at all.

I think one of the greatest things about marriage is that as both husband and father,
I can say anything I want to around the house. Of course, no one pays the least bit of attention.

A successful man is one who makes more money than his wife can spend.
A successful woman is one who can find such a man.

A man meets a genie. The genie tells him he can ask for whatever he wants, But his mother-in-law gets double of what he gets. The man thinks for a moment and says,
"Okay, give me a million dollars and beat me till I'm half dead."

How do most men define marriage?
An expensive way to get your laundry done free.

Words to live by: Do not argue with a spouse who is packing your parachute

First guy (proudly): "My wife's an angel!"
Second guy: "You're lucky, mine's still alive.

The most effective way to remember your wife's birthday is to forget it once.

Two old men were fishing off a bridge as they had done daily for many years.
Suddenly a funeral procession came down the road.
One old man reeled in his line, laid down his rod, faced the street and bowed his head until the procession had passed. He then picked up his rod and started fishing again.
The other fisherman was amazed and stated "I didn't know you were that religious.

" The other looked at him and said, "Least I could do, we was married for 42 years!"

One day an old poodle starts chasing butterflies in the African bush and before long,
he discovers that he's lost. Wandering about, he notices a leopard heading rapidly in his direction with the intention of having lunch.
The old poodle thinks, "Oh, oh! I'm in deep doo-doo now!" Noticing some bones on the ground close by, he immediately settles down to chew on the bones with his back to the approaching cat. Just as the leopard is about to leap the old poodle exclaims loudly, "Boy, that was one delicious leopard! I wonder if there are any more
around here"
Hearing this, the young leopard halts his attack in mid-strike, a look of terror comes over him and he slinks away into the trees.
"Whew!," Says the leopard, "That was close! That old poodle nearly had me!"
Meanwhile, a monkey who had been watching the whole scene from a nearby tree, figures he can put this knowledge to good use and trade it for protection from the leopard. So off he goes, but the old poodle sees Him heading after the leopard with great speed, and figures that something must be up. The monkey soon catches up with the leopard, spills the beans and strikes a deal for himself with the leopard.
The young leopard is furious at being made a fool of and says, "Here, Monkey, hop on my back and see what's going to happen to that conniving Canine!"
Now, the old poodle sees the leopard coming with the monkey on his back and thinks, "What am I going to do now?", but instead of running, the dog sits down with his back to his attackers, pretending he hasn't seen them yet, and just when they get close enough to hear, the old poodle says: "Where's that damn monkey? I sent him off an hour ago to bring me another leopard!"
Moral of this story...Don't mess with old farts...age and

treachery will always overcome youth and skill!
Bullshit and brilliance only come with age and experience!

ANAGRAMS

Dormitory = Dirty Room
Dictionary = Indicatory
Schoolmaster = The classroom
Elvis = Lives
Listen = Silent
Clint Eastwood = Old West Action
Western Union = No Wire Unsent
The country side = No City Dust Here
Evangelist = Evil's Agent
Postmaster = Stamp Store
A telescope = To see place
The eyes = They see
Waitress = A stew, Sir?
The centenarians = I can hear ten "tens"
Desperation = A rope ends it
I run to escape = A persecution
The Morse Code = Here Come Dots
Slot Machines = Cash Lost in'em
Conversation = Voices Rant On
Butterfly = Flutter-by
Heavy Rain? = Hire a Navy!
Mother-in-law = Woman Hitler
Father-in-law = Near halfwit
Funeral = Real Fun
A domesticated animal = Docile, as a man tamed it
The Railroad Train = Hi! I Rattle and Roar
Snooze Alarms = Alas! No More Z's
Vacation Times = I'm Not as Active

Vacation time = I am not active
The Detectives = Detect Thieves
The Hospital Ambulance = A Cab, I Hustle to Help Man
Semolina = Is No Meal
A Gentleman = Elegant Man
Presbyterians = Best In Prayers
The Public Art Galleries = Large Picture Halls, I Bet
A Decimal Point = I'm a Dot in Place
The Earthquakes = That Queer Shake
Statue of Liberty = Built to Stay Free
Eleven plus two = Twelve plus one
Patrick Stewart = A Crap Trek Twist
Admirer = Married
Indomitableness = Endless ambition
New York Times = Monkeys write
Television programming = Permeating living rooms
David Letterman = Nerd amid late TV
Howard Stern = Retard shown
Debit card = Bad credit

INSTANT PUT DOWNS & HECKLES

The reason you'd even call me that, tells me that you're ignorant, un-classy, and illiterate

I have way more important things to do than thinking about what you have to say to me.

You're not human, you're a black hole that sucks the life out of people, and I'm done with you.
I would insult you back but Mother Natures has already done such a fine job, I just couldn't compete.

I'm a lot better than what you have to look at in the mirror every morning

I thought I said goodbye to you this morning when I flushed the toilet

Funny you should call me an ugly bitch, your daddy likes to call me princess and other beautiful names, while he is dry humping my leg

I love it when you call me by your mom's name... Turns me on.

If you're trying to improve the world, you should start with yourself. Nothing needs more help than you do

I could eat a whole bowl of alphabet soup, shit it out, and have something better than u just said.

See ya and take care.. and by see ya I mean go fuck yourself and by take care I mean go fuck yourself.

People say laughter is the best medicine. Your face must be curing the world.

Sometimes the first step to forgiveness is understanding that the other person is a complete idiot.

You're spreading rumors about me? At least you found a hobby spreading something other than your legs.

the fact that jellyfish survived for 650 million years with no brains is good news for stupid people like you

Zombies are looking for brains. Don't worry. You're safe.

Somewhere out there is a tree, tirelessly producing oxygen so you can breath. I think you own it an apology

If you spoke your mind, you would be speechless

You remind me of a penny, two faced and f*cking worthless!

Keep rolling your eyes. Who knows, maybe you'll find a brain back there.

I was going to give you a nasty look but I see you already have one.

Someone gives you the middle finger* - "i have one of those too except i use it on your mom!"

I'd like to see things from your point of view but I can't seem to get my head that far up my ass.

In what chapter do you shut the f*ck up?

Everyone is entitled to be stupid, but you abuse the privilege.

I'd agree with you, but then we'd both be wrong.

I'm sorry what'd you say? I have an ear disease called I don't care.

I'm sorry I didn't get that.. I don't speak idiot

If you're going to be two faced, at least make on of them pretty

If you're gonna be a smartass, first you have to be smart. Otherwise you're just an ass.

Out of millions of sperm, you were the fastest?

Somewhere out there is a tree, tirelessly producing oxygen so you can breathe. I think you owe it an apology.

Hey, Rainman called. He wants his social skills back

Someone got up on the wrong side of the cage this morning

You should do some soul-searching. Maybe you'll find one.

I'm really easy to get along with once you people learn to see it my way.

If I throw a stick, will you leave?

I could say nice things about you, but I would rather tell the truth.

I know I'm talking like an idiot. I have to, other wise you wouldn't understand me.

I hope your day is as pleasant as you are.

I've been called worse things by better people.

I wish we could be better strangers.

There are two kinds of people in this world: people who care what you think, and people like me.

You're so dumb, your brain cell died of loneliness

Shouldn't you be out on a ledge somewhere?

You shouldn't let your mind wander..its way to small to be out on its own

I don't know what makes you so dumb, but its working

Next time you shave, try standing an inch or two closer to the blade

Wow that was a low blow! Speaking of low blows how's your mother

Unless your name is Google stop acting like you know everything

If you're waiting for me to care, you better pack a lunch. It's gonna be a while

You would be much more likable if it wasn't for that hole in your mouth that noise comes out of.

I'm fat because every time I did your mom she gave me a cookie

If you got a problem, take it up with my ass because that the only thing that give a crap

You should wear a condom on your head because if you're going act like a dick, you might as well dress like one

I'm sorry, talking with you sounds about as appealing as playing leapfrog with unicorns

I can't seem to find my dick.. mind if I look in your mothers mouth

I refuse to engage in a battle of wits as I will not take advantage of the handicapped

Some babies were dropped on their heads but clearly you were thrown at the wall

Life is like toilet paper, you're either on a role or your taking shit from some asshole

Why do you keep coming back to me? You're like herpes

What died on your neck? Oh, it's your head

Why don't you shut up and give that hole in your face a chance to heal

If you had any intelligence to question I would have questioned it already.

I wish I had a lower I.Q, maybe then I could enjoy your company.

I don't have the time or energy to sink to your level; you have a nice day though.

I would answer you back but life is too short, just like your d*ck

Mirrors don't lie. Lucky for you, they can't laugh either.

Were you always this stupid or did you take lessons

Don't talk about yourself so much ... we'll do that when you leave

What do you do if you come across a tiger in the jungle? Wipe it off and apologise

New Miley Cyrus DVD: £15
Extra large box of tissues: £2
The look of disgust on the cashier's face as you pay: priceless

I went to see the nurse this morning for my annual checkup.
She told me that I have to stop wanking.
I asked, "why?"
She replied, "because I'm trying to examine you"

Nothing says "almost caught masturbating" like having your mom walk in on you looking at the Google homepage

What's the most sensitive part of your body when you're having a wank?
Your ears

Looks aren't everything, but you can't wank over personality

My wife said, "why is the laptop all sticky?"
I said, "it's not what you think, it's ice cream,"
She said, "how did you manage to get ice cream all over the laptop?"
I said, "have you ever tried eating an ice cream whilst masturbating?"

I wanked over a blind girl the other day. She didn't see me coming

FIVE MINUTE MANAGEMENT COURSE

Lesson 1:

A man has just gotten into the shower as his wife is stepping out of the shower, when the doorbell rings.

The wife quickly wraps herself in a towel and runs downstairs.

When she opens the door, there stands Bob, their next-door neighbour.

Before she says a word, Bob says, 'I'll give you £800 to drop that towel.'

After thinking for a moment, the woman drops her towel and stands naked in front of Bob, after a few seconds, Bob hands her £800 and leaves.

The woman wraps back up in the towel and goes back upstairs.

When she gets to the bathroom, her husband asks, 'Who was that?'

'It was Bob, from next door.' she replies.

'Great,' the husband says, 'did he say anything about the £800 he owes me?'

Moral of the story:

If you share critical information pertaining to credit and risk with your shareholders in time, you may be in a position to prevent avoidable exposure.

Lesson 2:

A priest offered a nun a lift.

She got in and crossed her legs, forcing her habit to reveal a leg.

The priest nearly had an accident.

After controlling the car, he stealthily slid his hand up her leg.

The nun said, 'Father, remember Psalm 129?'

The priest removed his hand. But, changing gears, he let his hand slide up her leg again.

The nun once again said, 'Father, remember Psalm 129?'

The priest apologised 'Sorry sister, but the flesh is weak.'

Arriving at the convent, the nun sighed heavily and went on her way.

On his arrival at the church, the priest rushed to look up Psalm 129. It said, 'Go forth and seek, further up, you will find glory.'

Moral of the story:

If you are not well informed in your job, you might miss a great opportunity.

Lesson 3:

A sales rep, an administration clerk, and their manager are walk-

J. J. WILKINSON

ing to lunch when they find an antique oil lamp.

They rub it and a Genie comes out.

The Genie says, 'I'll give each of you just one wish.'

'Me first! Me first!' says the admin clerk. 'I want to be in the Bahamas, driving a speedboat, without a care in the world.'

Puff! She's gone.

'Me next! Me next!' says the sales rep. 'I want to be in Hawaii, relaxing on the beach with my personal masseuse, an endless supply of Pina Coladas and the love of my life.'

Puff! He's gone.

'OK, you're up,' the Genie says to the manager.

The manager says, 'I want those two back in the office after lunch.'

Moral of the story:

Always let your boss have the first say.

Lesson 4

An eagle was sitting on a tree resting, doing nothing.

A small rabbit saw the eagle and asked him, 'Can I also sit like you and do nothing?'

The eagle answered: 'Sure, why not.'

So, the rabbit sat on the ground below the eagle and rested.

All of a sudden, a fox appeared, jumped on the rabbit and ate it.

Moral of the story:

114

JOKES TO KEEP YOU OCCUPIED DURING ISOLATION

To be sitting and doing nothing, you must be sitting very, very high up.

Lesson 5

A turkey was chatting with a bull.

'I would love to be able to get to the top of that tree' sighed the turkey, 'but I haven't got the energy.'

'Well, why don't you nibble on some of my droppings?' replied the bull. They're packed with nutrients.'

The turkey pecked at a lump of dung, and found it actually gave him enough strength to reach the lowest branch of the tree.

The next day, after eating some more dung, he reached the second branch.

Finally after a fourth night, the turkey was proudly perched at the top of the tree.

He was promptly spotted by a farmer, who shot him out of the tree.

Moral of the story:

Bull shit might get you to the top, but it won't keep you there.

Lesson 6

A little bird was flying south for the winter. It was so cold the bird froze and fell to the ground in a large field.

While he was lying there, a cow came by and dropped some dung on him.

As the frozen bird lay there in the pile of cow dung, he began to realise how warm he was.

The dung was actually thawing him out!

He lay there all warm and happy, and soon began to sing for joy. A passing cat heard the bird singing and came to investigate.

Following the sound, the cat discovered the bird under the pile of cow dung, and promptly dug him out and ate him.

Morals of the story:

(1) Not everyone who shits on you is your enemy.

(2) Not everyone who gets you out of shit is your friend.

(3) And when you're in deep shit, it's best to keep your mouth shut!

THUS ENDS THE FIVE MINUTE MANAGEMENT COURSE

TIME TO CRINGE

The wife has been missing a week now. Police said to prepare for the worst. So I have been to the charity shop to get all her clothes back.

I was explaining to my wife last night that when you die you get reincarnated but must come back as a different creature. She said "I would like to come back as a cow". I said "you're obviously not listening".

Doctors have just identified a food that can cause grief and suffering years after it's been eaten. No it's not Cucumber!
It's called a wedding cake.

Man calls 999 and says "I think my wife is dead" The operator says how do you know? He says "The sex is the same but the ironing is building up"!

I saw this bloke chatting up a cheetah, I thought, "he's trying to pull a fast one".

So I said to this train driver, "I want to go to Paris." He said, "Eurostar?" I said, "I've been on the telly but I'm no Dean Martin".

So I said to the gym instructor, "Can you teach me to do the splits?" He said, "How flexible are you?" I said, "I can't make Tuesdays".

So I was having dinner with Gary Kasparov and there was a checked tablecloth. It took him two hours to pass me the salt.

He said, "You remind me of a pepper-pot." I said, "I'll take that as a condiment".

Do you know I've got a friend who's fallen in love with two school bags? He's bisatchel.

But I'll tell you what I love doing more than anything: trying to pack myself in a small suitcase. I can hardly contain myself.

Now you know those trick candles that you blow out and a couple of seconds later they come alight again? Well, the other day there was a fire at the factory that makes them.

So I met this gangster who pulls up the back of people's pants, it was Weggie Kray. So I said, "Do you want a game of darts?" He said, "OK then." I said, "Nearest to bull starts." He said, "Baa." I said, "Moo." He said, "You're closest".

You see I'm against hunting. In fact, I'm a hunt saboteur. I go out the night before and shoot the fox.

The other day I sent my girlfriend a huge pile of snow. I rang her up, I said, "Do you get my drift"?

So I went down the local supermarket, I said, "I want to make a complaint -- this vinegar's got lumps in it." He said, "Those are pickled onions".

So I went to the Chinese restaurant and this duck came up to me with a red rose and says, "Your eyes sparkle like diamonds." I said, "Waiter, I asked for a-ROMATIC duck".

But I'm in great mood tonight because the other day I entered a competition and I won a years supply of Marmite ... one jar.

So this bloke says to me, "Can I come in your house and talk about your carpets?" I thought, "That's all I need, a Je-hoover's witness".

You see my next-door neighbour worships exhaust pipes. He's a Catholic converter.

So I rang up British Telecom, I said, "I want to report a nuisance caller." He said, "Not you again".

So I was in Tesco's and I saw this man and woman wrapped in a barcode. I said, "Are you two an item"?

So a lorry-load of tortoises crashed into a train-load of terrapins. I thought, "That's a turtle disaster".

I just got off the phone to Sea World... My call was recorded for training porpoises.

I think our new pet Rabbit must be vicious... The wife said when she brings it home I'm going to have to make a run for it

Just had a good tip 4 the grand national... A horse called creosote..! Goes really wel over fences...!!

I changed my iPod's name to Titanic... It's syncing now.

When chemists die... They barium.

Jokes about German sausage... Are the wurst.

I know a guy who's addicted to brake fluid... He says he can stop any time.

How does Moses make his tea? Hebrews it.

I stayed up all night to see where the sun went... Then it dawned on me.

A girl said she recognized me from the vegetarian club but I'd never met herbivore.

I'm reading a book about anti-gravity... I just can't put it down.

I did a theatrical performance about puns... It was a play on words.

They told me I had type-A blood but it was a Type-O.

PMS jokes aren't funny; period.

Why were the Indians here first? They had reservations.

We're going on a class trip to the Coca-Cola factory. I hope there's no pop quiz.

I didn't like my beard at first. Then it grew on me.

Did you hear about the cross-eyed teacher who lost her job because she couldn't control her pupils?

When you get a bladder infection urine trouble.

Broken pencils are pointless.

I tried to catch some fog, but I mist.

What do you call a dinosaur with an extensive vocabulary? A thesaurus.

England has no kidney bank, but it does have a Liverpool.

I used to be a banker, but then I lost interest.

I dropped out of communism class because of lousy Marx.

All the toilets in New York's police stations have been stolen. The police have nothing to go on.

I got a job at a bakery because I kneaded dough.

Haunted French pancakes give me the crêpes.

Velcro — what a rip off!

A cartoonist was found dead in his home. Details are sketchy.

Venison for dinner again? Oh deer!

The earthquake in Washington obviously was the government's fault.

Be kind to your dentist. He has fillings, too.

How many of you believe in telekinesis? Raise MY hand!

Wife: "I look fat. Can you give me a compliment?" Husband: "You have perfect eyesight."

Where do they get the seeds to plant seedless watermelons?

I was born to be a pessimist. My blood type is B Negative.

You sound reasonable. It must be time to up my medication!

Doing things that you are not supposed to do at work makes your vision, hearing and alertness much better.

I'm emotionally constipated. I haven't given a shit in days.

You know you're ugly when it comes to a group picture and they hand you the camera.

What is the difference between men and women? A woman wants one man to satisfy her every need...A man wants every woman to satisfy his one need.

My New Year's resolution is to help all my friends gain ten pounds so I look skinnier.

Depression is merely anger without enthusiasm.

My psychiatrist said I was pre-occupied with the vengeance I told him "oh yeah we'll see about that!"

Always identify who to blame in an emergency.

I think the most exciting thing about being an adult is never knowing what part of your body is going to hurt the next day

Crime doesn't pay... does that mean that my job is a crime?

I'm at a McDonalds and their phone just rang. I have to assume whoever is making that call is a completely unstable human being.

Your future depends on your dreams. Don't waste any time, go to bed now.

You must have been born on a highway because that's where most accidents happen.

There may be no excuse for laziness, but I'm still looking.

My wife was furious at me for kicking dropped ice cubes under the refrigerator. But now it's just water under the fridge.

Evening news is where they begin with 'Good evening', and then proceed to tell you why it isn't.

I'm an adult. I don't cry over spilt milk unless it has coffee in it.

Politicians and diapers have one thing in common. They should both be changed regularly, and for the same reason.

If a child refuses to sleep during nap time, are they guilty of resisting a rest?

Why did the blonde snort artificial sweetener? She thought it was diet coke.

The trouble with being punctual is that nobody's there to appreciate it.

You know that tingly little feeling you get when you like someone? That's your common sense leaving your body.

Currently the flower business is blooming.

How does Moses make his tea? Hebrews it.

This morning some clown opened the door for me. I thought to myself that's a nice Jester.

Adults are always asking little kids what they want to be when they grow up because they're looking for ideas.

Life isn't about winning and losing. It's about wishing you would have won and wondering why you lost.

Latest survey shows that 3 out of 4 people make up 75% of the world's population.

Give me ambiguity or give me something else.

Sometimes I wake up grumpy; other times I let her sleep.

We live in an age where mentioning you read a book seems a little bit like you're showing off.

What color do Smurfs turn if you choke them?

If you don't care where you are, then you ain't lost.

Every time I find the meaning of life, they change it.

If you enjoy arguing about lunches at 6 AM I can't recommend parenting highly enough.

You're so ugly, when your mom dropped you off at school she got a fine for littering.

I'm blonde. What's your excuse?

How do you drown a blonde? Put a scratch and sniff at the bottom of the bathtub.

I don't think it's possible for me to become a sniper. Not by a long shot.

It's not the fall that kills you; it's the sudden stop at the end.

Take my advice — I'm not using it.

By working faithfully eight hours a day you may eventually get to be boss and work twelve hours a day.

The downside of dating intelligent women is having to Google the names they call you when it ends badly.

Becoming a parent is great. It's a beautiful and rewarding experience. It's almost as good as not becoming one.

Children are the leading cause of old age.

I am depressed in every way except emotionally.

Most people are shocked when they find out how bad I am as an electrician

Do I know you? Cause you look a lot like my next girlfriend.

I'm changing my name to 'Benefits' on Facebook. Next time someone adds me, It will say "you are now friends with Benefits."

Children seldom misquote you. In fact, they usually repeat word for word what you shouldn't have said.

The light at the end of the tunnel has been turned off due to budget cuts.

What's the difference between your wife and your job? After five years your job will still suck.

Did you hear about the 2 silk worms in a race? It ended in a tie!

I hate peer pressure and you should too.

"I'm sorry" and "I apologize" mean the same thing... except when you're at a funeral.

A friend of mine tried to annoy me with bird puns, but I soon realized that toucan play at that game.

Why couldn't the bike stand up on it's own? It was two tired.

I feel like I'm diagonally parked in a parallel universe.

They tell you that you'll lose your mind when you grow older. What they don't tell you is that you won't miss it very much.

Why didn't the man report his stolen credit card? The thief was spending less then his wife.

What's a mixed feeling? When you see your mother-in-law backing off a cliff in your new car.

When I get naked in the bathroom, the shower usually gets turned on.

My first job was working in an orange juice factory, but I got canned: couldn't concentrate.

It is very easy to become a superman, you just have to change the sequence of clothes while wearing.

It turns out the answer to my problems wasn't at the bottom of this pint of ice cream, but the important thing is that I tried.

I bought a box of condoms earlier today. The cashier asked if I'd like a bag. I said "nah, I'll just turn the lights off."

If love is blind, why is lingerie so popular?

You never realize what you have until it's gone. Toilet paper, for example.

I have to exercise early in the morning before my brain figures out what I'm doing.

Never, under any circumstances, take a sleeping pill and a laxative on the same night.

Hard work has a future payoff. Laziness pays off now.

If you can stay calm while all around you is chaos, then you probably haven't completely understood the situation.

Ok, what's the latest possible date that I can still make something of my life?

A mate said he saw several elderly men repairing shoes in the back of a van. I reckon it's a load of old cobblers.

If you find yourself in a hole. Stop digging.

Congratulations, If you press the elevator button three times it goes into hurry mode – really...

My favorite mythical creature? The honest politician.

I had a job tying sausages together, but I couldn't make ends meet.

My math teacher called me average. How mean!

A book just fell on my head. I've only got myshelf to blame.

I'd like to see things from your point of view but I can't seem to get my head that far up my ass.

Hard work never killed anyone, but why take the chance?

I walked past a homeless guy with a sign that read, "One day, this could be you." I put my money back in my pocket, just in case he's right.

I always wanted to marry an Archeologist. The older I would get, the more interested she would become!

I'm trying to date a philosophy professor, but she doesn't even know if I exist or not.

I asked my wife why she never blinked during foreplay. She said she didn't have time.

I tried to escape the Apple store. I couldn't because there were no Windows.

I'm jealous of all the people that haven't met you!

My girlfriend and I often laugh about how competitive we are. But I laugh more.

My wife and I always compromise. I admit I'm wrong and she agrees with me.

What's the best part about Valentine's Day? The day after when all the chocolate goes on sale.

I love how in horror movies the person will ask, "Is anyone there?" As if the killer would say "Oh yeah I'm in the kitchen. Want a sandwich?"

By the time a man realises that his father was right, he has a son who thinks he's wrong.

My aunt's star sign was cancer, pretty ironic how she died. She was eaten by a giant crab.

I intend to live forever... or die trying.

Well son, in the '90s, there was no drooling emoji. You had to show up at a girl's door and actually drool.

One of the benefits of eating healthier is that you never have to ask questions like, "Who ate my salad?"

Good morning to everyone except people who call to make sure you got their email (like 30 seconds after you got it).

Despite my specific instructions, no one that has listened to my voicemail has left me a massage after the beep.

To err is human, to blame it on somebody else shows management potential.

What is an astronaut's favorite key on a keyboard? Space!

It takes patience to listen.. it takes skill to pretend you're listening.

Being a hypochondriac is going to save my life one of these days

I am on a seafood diet. Every time I see food, I eat it.

I have an inferiority complex but it's not a very good one.

Just remember, it's better to pay full price than to admit you're a senior citizen.

You can tell a girl likes you if she stares at your phone instead of her own.

Never get on one knee for a girl who won't get on two for you.

There's nothing like the joy on a kid's face when he first sees the PlayStation box containing the socks I got him for Christmas.

The last airline I flew charged for everything. Except for the bad service. That was free.

If you do not say it, they can't repeat it.

I just got this sick job at the Calendar factory. Unfortunately, I still can't get a date.

It looks like your face caught on fire and someone tried to put it out with a hammer.

Loneliness is when a person always knows where all of his things are.

I wasn't born with enough middle fingers to let you know how I feel about you.

Three conspiracy theorists walk into a bar. You can't tell me that's just a coincidence!

Books are just TV for smart people.

I like birthdays, but I think too many can kill you.

There's only one problem with your face, I can see it.

I hate cocaine dealers. Always sticking their business into other people's noses.

Never tell a woman that her place is in the kitchen. That's where the knives are kept.

I've never understood how the Nazis couldn't find where Anne Frank was hiding. I've been to Amsterdam... There are signs pointing to her house everywhere.

They say you are what you eat, so lay off the nuts.

Never tell your problems to anyone...20% don't care and the other 80% are glad you have them...

The trouble with learning from experience is that you never graduate.

If I ever need a heart transplant, I'd want my ex's. It's never been used.

Change is inevitable, except from a vending machine.

Living on earth may be expensive, but it includes an annual free trip around the sun.

Girls are like roads, more the curves, more the dangerous they are.

The doctor told his patient to stop using a Q-tip, but it went in one ear and out the other.

Wifi went down during family dinner tonight. One kid started talking and I didn't know who he was.

The first time I got a universal remote control, I thought to myself "This changes everything".

I sat next to a man on the park bench. He had 9 watches on one wrist and 5 in the other. I said man "you sure do have a lot of time on your hands."

As I get older and remember all the people I've lost along the way. I think to myself maybe a career as a tour guide wasn't for me.

We are born naked, wet and hungry. Then things get worse.

My wife is going to qualify for free shipping no matter how much it costs.

I got a job in a health club, but they said I wasn't fit for the job.

You are proof that evolution CAN go in reverse.

So, a thought crossed your mind? Must have been a long and lonely journey.

Hey, you have something on your chin... no, the 3rd one down.

Top 3 situations that require witnesses:

1) Crimes
2) Accidents
3) Marriages

Need I say more?

Never break someone's heart because they have only one inside... break their bones because they have 206 of them.

Did you hear about the Italian chef with a terminal illness? He past away.

The human brain is one of the most complex objects in the universe. Is it any wonder that so many people never learn to use it.

There is no key to a woman's heart. There's only a password that changes regularly.

Why was the tree excited about the future? It was ready to turn over a new leaf!

Everywhere is walking distance if you have the time.

Confucius say, man who runs behind car will get exhausted, but man who runs in front of car will get tired.

I'm not saying I hate you, but I would unplug your life support to charge my phone.

The difference between "Girlfriend" and "Girl Friend" is that little space in between we call the "Friend Zone".

I'm not lazy... I'm just on my energy saving mode.

If tomatoes are technically a fruit, is ketchup technically a smoothie?

Teacher: "Which book has helped you the most in your life?"
Student: "My father's cheque book!"

What happened when the semicolon broke grammar laws? It was given two consecutive sentences.

Refusing to go to the gym counts as resistance training, right?

We never really grow up, we only learn how to act in public.

The sole purpose of a child's middle name, is so he can tell when he's really in trouble.

A guy goes to a club; the bouncer stops him. "No tie, no entry." He walks back to his car to find a tie. All he found were jumper cables so he puts them around his neck like a tie. He goes back and says "How's this?" The bouncer says "I'll let you in, but don't start anything."

If you think nobody cares if you're alive, try missing a couple of payments.

Be careful of your thoughts, they may become words at any moment.

Shin: A device for finding furniture in the dark.

Somebody stole my mood ring and I'm not quite sure how I feel about that..

The nurse at the sperm bank asked me if I'd like to masturbate in the cup. I said, "Well, I'm pretty good, but I don't think I'm ready to compete just yet."

One day I'll look up from my phone and realize my kids put me in a nursing home.

I received a call from the school telling me my son is constantly lying. I said "Tell him he's a good liar. I don't have a son."

Diplomacy is the art of letting someone else get your way.

I'm gonna spend Valentine's Day with my ex... Box 360.

How did they invent break dancing? Trying to steal the hubcaps off a moving car.

Retirement kills more people than hard work ever did.

What's the definition of a surprise? A fart with a lump in it.

There are two rules for success: 1) Don't tell all you know.

If winning isn't everything why do they keep score?

Statistically 6 out of 7 Dwarfs are not Happy.

What do prisoners use to call each other? Cell phones.

What is the best Christmas present ever? A broken drum - you can't beat it!

My calling in life went straight to voicemail.

A procrastinator's work is never done.

Never answer an anonymous letter.

I just found an origami porn channel, but it is paper view only.

Nothing ruins a Friday more than an understanding that today is Tuesday.

Going to attempt a Mexican joke. Hope it's a good Juan!

Did you hear about the hungry clock? It went back four seconds!

What is the name of an Asian pilot who died in a plane crash? Sum Ting Wong.

My first child has gone off to college and I feel a great emptiness in my life. Specifically, in my checking account.

Transitional age is when during a hot day you don't know what you want – ice cream or beer.

Why do women love Chinese food? Because WON TON spelled backward is NOT NOW!

Oh, what? Sorry. I was trying to imagine you with a personality.

My mother never saw the irony in calling me a son-of-a-bitch.

Remember, children. The best way to get a puppy for Christmas is to beg for a baby brother.

I like you. You remind me of when I was young and stupid.

The trouble with unemployment is that the minute you wake up in the morning you're on the job.

Honesty is the best policy but insanity is the best defense.

For every action there is an equal and opposite criticism.

Why was the horse so happy? Because he lived in a stable environment.

Don't steal. That's the government's job.

Do you believe in love at first sight or do i pass by you again.

My buddy set me up on a blind date & said, "Heads up, she's expecting a baby." Felt like an idiot sitting in the bar wearing just a diaper.

My love is like communism; everyone gets a share, and it's only good in theory.

It is much easier to apologize than to ask permission.

I used to work at a fire hydrant factory couldn't park nowhere near the place.

Aha, I see the Fuck-Up Fairy has visited us again!

I don't think you act stupid, I'm sure it's the real thing.

What makes men chase women they have no intention of marrying? The same urge that makes dogs chase cars they have no intention of driving.

My bed wasn't feeling well this morning, so I had to stay home to take care of it.

Why call someone when you can just decide where you and your friend want to meet by exchanging 76 text messages?

How come "you're a peach" is a complement but "you're bananas" is an insult? Why are we allowing fruit discrimination to tear society apart?

My wife pissed me off in my dream. When I woke up and told her about it she said it was probably something I started so I ended up apologizing and bought her flowers.

If Barbie is so popular, why do you have to buy her friends?

I would ask you how old you are but I know you can't count that high.

Everyone has a photographic memory, some don't have film.

I hate insects puns, they really bug me.

Q: What did one ocean say to the other ocean?
A: Nothing, they just waved.

Education is important but other stuff is more importanter.

I went to buy some camouflage trousers the other day but I couldn't find any.

I would give my right arm to be ambidextrous!

I got in a fight one time with a really big guy, and he said, "I'm going to mop the floor with your face." I said, "You'll be sorry." He said, "Oh, yeah? Why?" I said, "Well, you won't be able to get into the corners very well."

By the time you learn the rules of life, you're too old to play the game.

I always adjust the seat and mirrors when I drive my husband's car so he doesn't forget he's married.

Why didn't Cupid shoot his arrow at the lawyer's heart? Because even Cupid can't hit a target that small.

What is a baptized Mexican called? Bean dip.

I WRITE ALL MY JOKES IN CAPITALS. THIS ONE WAS WRITTEN IN PARIS.

How can you spot the blind guy at the nudist colony? It's not hard.

I'm not a doctor but I know adding cheese to anything makes it an antidepressant.

I've reached the age where looking in the mirror is like checking the news. I know there'll be some new developments I won't like.

My ex texted me: Can you delete my number? I responded: Who is this?

Knowledge is knowing a tomato is a fruit; Wisdom is not putting it in a fruit salad.

I once worked as a salesman and was very independent; I took orders from no one.

I am busy contemplating my future. Don't worry, this will only take a minute.

Hippopotomonstrosesquippedaliophobia: Fear of long words.

Why did the duck go to rehab? Because he was a quack addict!

We all have one ginger friend that claims to be "strawberry blonde".

Sang the rainbow song in front of a police officer, got arrested for colourful language

Remember, everyone seems normal until you get to know them...

Playing with a toddler is half play and half self-defense.

Every time someone calls me fat I get so depressed I cut myself... a piece of cake.

I had prepared for a battle of wits but I see you came unarmed.

Accidentally pooped my pants in the elevator. I'm taking this shit to a whole new level.

Why do Retirees smile all the time? Because they can't hear a word you're saying!

If you really want to know about mistakes, you should ask your parents.

You're not old until a teenager describes you as middle-aged.

"Doctor, I'm addicted to 'The Family Feud' game show. What's wrong with me?
Doctor: "Well, the survey says..."

You know your children are growing up when they stop asking you where they came from and refuse to tell you where they're going.

Brains aren't everything. In your case they're nothing.

We can always tell when you are lying. Your lips move.

You're so fake, Barbie is jealous.

Why is "abbreviation" such a long word?

My landlord says he needs to come talk to me about how high my heating bill is. I told him, "My door is always open".

It's hard to explain puns to kleptomaniacs because they always take things literally.

Early to bed, early to rise makes people suspicious.

I was going to give him a nasty look, but he already had one.

Any room is a panic room if you've lost your phone in it.

My boss told me to have a good day. So I went home.

If the speed of light is 186,000 miles/sec., what's the speed of darkness?

If your wife wants to learn to drive, don't stand in her way.

What's the best place to grow flowers in school?... In the kinder-garden.

I am a nobody, nobody is perfect, therefore I am perfect.

I've put something aside for a rainy day. It's an umbrella.

Working at a Hospital is the worst cause you can't call in sick. You: "Yeah, I can't come in today, I'm sick." Boss: "Come on in, we'll check you out."

There's never enough time to do it right, but there's always enough time to do it over.

Two dogs are walking along a street. They are passed by a third dog driving a lorry load of logs. One turns to the other and says: "He started fetching a stick and built up the business from there."

What do sea monsters eat for lunch? Fish and ships.

XXX & OFFENSIVE

What's the difference between a blonde and a mosquito?
A mosquito stops sucking when you smack it.

How is a pussy like a grapefruit?
The best ones squirt when you eat them.

What's the difference between acne and a Catholic Priest?
Acne will usually not come on a kid's face until around 13 or 14 years of age.

How do you turn a fox into an elephant?
Marry it!

Why does the bride always wear white?
Because it is good for the dishwasher to match the stove and refrigerator.

What is the difference between a battery and a woman?
A battery has a positive side.

How do you tell if a chick's too fat to f*ck?
When you pull her pants down and her ass is still in them.

What is the difference between a drug dealer and a hooker?
A hooker can wash her crack and sell it again!

Do you know why they call it the Wonder Bra?
When you take it off you wonder where her tits went.

Why is it so hard for women to take a piss in the morning?
Did you ever try to peel apart a grilled cheese sandwich?

Why don't pygmies wear tampons?
They keep stepping on the strings.

What do you call 25 lesbians stacked on top of each other?
A block of flaps!

How do we know God is a man?
Because if God were a woman, sperm would taste like chocolate!

Why do women rub their eyes when they get up in the morning?
They don't have balls to scratch.

What is the definition of making love?
Something a woman does while a guy is humping her

What's the best thing about Alzheimer's disease?
You get to meet new people every day!

Why is it difficult to find men who are sensitive, caring and good looking?
They've got boyfriends already.

Why do women close their eyes during sex?
They can't stand seeing a man have a good time.

Why do men like blowjobs?
It's the only time they get something into a woman's head straight!

What's the biggest problem for an atheist?
No-one to talk to during an orgasm!

What's worse than a cardboard box?
Paper tits!

Why do Jewish men like to watch porno movies backwards?
They like the part where the hooker gives the money back.

What is 60 foot long and stinks of piss?
A conga in an old people's home!

Why are electric trains like a mother's breasts?
They were both designed for the kids, but it's the fathers who are always playing with them.

What do women & dog turds have in common?
The older they are, the easier they are to pick up!

What is the similarity between a woman and laxative?
They both irritate the shit out of you!

What's the best thing about a blow job?
Five minutes of peace and quiet.

What's the difference between Bill Clinton and JFK?
One got his head blown off and the other was assassinated.

What's the difference between a lawyer and God?
God doesn't think he's a lawyer

What's the difference between toilet paper and toast?
Toast is brown on both sides.

What's the medical term for a female-to-male sex change operation?
Strapadictomy.

Two condoms walk past a gay bar. One of them says to the other, "Hey, whaddya say we go in there & get shit-faced? "

What do you call three dogs and a blackbird?
The Spice Girls

What's the similarity between getting a blow job from an eighty year-old and walking the tightrope?
In both cases you really don't want to look down...

What's the difference between a dog and a fox?
About eight pints of beer.

How do you embarrass an archaeologist?
Give him a used tampon and ask him which period it's from.

What's the difference between love, true love
and showing off?
Spitting, swallowing and gargling
What's the difference between a Catholic wife and a Jewish wife?
A Catholic wife has real orgasms and fake jewelry.

What makes men chase women they have no intention of marrying?
The same urge that makes dogs chase cars they have no intention of driving.

Who is the most popular guy at the nudist colony?
The guy who can carry a cup of coffee in each hand and a dozen donuts.

Who is the most popular girl at the nudist colony?
She is the one who can eat the last donut!

The three words most hated by men during sex?
"Are you In?" or "Is It In? "

Three words women hate to hear when having sex
"Honey, I'm home!"

Why do men take showers instead of baths?
Pissing in the bath is disgusting.

Did you hear about the new paint called "Blonde" paint?
It's not very bright, but it spreads easy.

What is sometimes hard, sometimes soft and combines with crumpet to give pleasure?
Butter.

What's big, purple and swims in the sea?
Moby Plum

What do you call the crusties inside of women's underwear?
Clitty litter.

What should you do if you find your husband staggering in the backyard?
Shoot him again.

Did you hear about the two blondes that were found frozen to death in their car at the drive in?
Yeah, they went to see "Closed For The Winter"

What should you do if you girlfriend starts smoking?
Slow down and use a lubricant.

What do you call the useless piece of skin on the end of a man's penis?
His body.

How can you tell when a man is well-hung?
When you can just barely slip your finger in between his neck and the noose.

Why do little boys whine?
Because they're practicing to be men.

How many men does it take to screw in a light bulb?
One – he just holds it up there and waits for the world to revolve around him

How many men does it take to screw in a light bulb?

Three – one to screw in the bulb, and two to listen to him brag about the screwing part.
What do you call a handcuffed man?
Trustworthy.

What does it mean when a man is in your bed gasping for breath and calling your name?
You didn't hold the pillow down long enough.

Why do doctors slap babies butts right after they're born?
To knock the penises off the smart ones.

Why do men name their penises?
Because they don't like the idea of having a stranger make 90% of their decisions.

Why does it take 100,000,000 sperm to fertilize one egg?
Because not one will stop and ask directions.

Why do female black widow spiders kill their males after mating?
To stop the snoring before it starts.

What's the best way to kill a man?
Put a naked woman and a six-pack in front of him. Then tell him to pick only one.

What do men and pantyhose have in common?
They either cling, run or don't fit right in the crotch!

What is the difference between men and women?
A woman wants one man to satisfy her every need. A man wants every woman to satisfy his one need.

How does a man keep his youth?
By giving her money, furs and diamonds.

How do you keep your husband from reading your e-mail?
Rename the mail folder to "instruction manuals"

What is the best thing to come out of Wales?

The M4.

Did you hear about the man who was tap dancing?
He broke his ankle when he fell into the sink.

"Doctor, doctor. Every time I sit down, I see visions of Mickey Mouse and Pluto, every time I stand up, I see Donald Duck."
"How long have you been having these Disney spells?"

An Irishman goes up to bed every night taking a full glass of water and an empty glass with him .Why?
Because some nights he is thirsty, and some nights he isn't.

What do you say to a woman with no arms and no legs? Nice tits!

What's the difference between a blonde and an ironing board?
It's difficult to open the legs of an ironing board.

How does every ethnic joke start?
By looking over your shoulder.

What do you call a man with two raincoats on in a cemetary?
Max Bygraves
When is a pixie not a pixie?
When he's got his head up a fairy's skirt, then he's a goblin'.

What's the difference between light and hard?
You can get to sleep with a light on.

What do you call a man with a seagull on his head?
Cliff

Why did the man cross the road?
He heard the chicken was a slut.

What do women and prawns have in common?
Their heads are full of shit but the pink bits taste great.

What do you call a woman with one leg shorter than the other?
Eileen

How many pessimists does it take to change a light bulb?

None, it's probably screwed in too tight anyway.

How many Freudian analysts does it take to cange a light bulb?
Two, one to change the bulb and one to hold the penis, I mean ladder.

What's the definition of "trust"?
Two cannibals giving each other a blowjob.

Confucious he say...
Man who drive like hell bound to get there!

What's got 90 balls and makes women sweat?
Bingo.

What's the difference between a hormone and an enzyme?
You can't hear an enzyme

Clinton's artful denial: "I didn't put words in her mouth."

What do you call a man who's been underground for 100 years?
Pete

What did the egg say to the boiling water?
"It might take me a while to get hard I just got laid last night."

Confucious he say...
Man who drop watch in toilet have shitty time.

Confucious he say...
Man who stand on toilet high on pot.

What does DNA stand for?
National Association of Dyslexics.

Being punctual in our Office was of no benefit what-so-ever.
There was never anybody around to appreciate it.

Confucious he say...
Passionate kiss like spider web – soon lead to undoing of fly.

What do you call a man with a shovel on his head?

Doug

How many honest, intelligent, caring men in the world does it take to do the dishes?
Both of them.

Why should you never make love to a female astronaut twice?
You might burn up on re-entry

How are men and parking spots alike?
Good ones are always taken. Free ones are mostly handicapped or extremely small.

What do you call a man with no arms and no legs swimming in the sea?
Bob

How many animals can you fit in a pair of stockings?
Two Calves, an ass, a pussy, and god knows how many hairs.

What's green and gets you pissed?
A Giro

Make it idiot proof and someone will make a better idiot.

Confucious he say...
Man who eat many prunes get good run for money.

One day as I came home early from work ..... I saw a guy jogging naked. Said to the guy, "hey buddy .... why are you doing that?"
He said, "because you came home early."

Confucious he say...
Man who run behind car get exhausted. Man who run in front of car get tired.

Why did God create Eve?
Well somebody had to iron Adam's leaf.

What is the definition of Confidence?
When your wife catches you in bed with another woman and you

slap her on the ass and say, "You're next!"

Confucious he say...
Man who fart in church must sit in own pew.

Confucious he say...
Foolish man give wife grand piano. Wise man give wife upright organ.

Why do chickens raise one leg when they sleep?
Because if they lifted both, they'd fall over.

Confucious he say...
War not determine who right. War determine who left.

Why don't women blink during foreplay?
They don't have time.
How many social workers does it take to change a light bulb?
None, but it takes 15 to write a paper entitled "coping with darkness"

What is the difference between a frog and a horny toad?
One says ribbit ribbit, the other one says rub-it rub it!

Why are married women heavier than single women?
Single women come home, see what's in the fridge and go to bed. Married women come home, see what's in bed and go to the fridge.

What do breasts and train sets have in common?
They were both designed for babies, but are played with by men.

How did Pinocchio find out he was made of wood?
His hand caught fire.

What's the difference between a dead dog in the road and a dead lawyer in the road?
There are skid marks in front of the dog.

What do you call a woman with tiles on her head?
Ruth

What do you do if your boiler explodes?
Buy her some flowers.

What do you call a woman playing pool whilst balancing two pints of lager on her head?
Beatrix Potter

Confucious he say...
Wife who put husband in doghouse soon find him in cathouse.

How do you know when you are getting old?
When you start having dry dreams and wet farts.

Why does it take 1 million sperm to fertilise one egg?
They won't stop to ask directions.

How does a man show that he is planning for the future?
He buys two cases of beer.

What do you call a man with a car on his head?
Jack

Why are there no ashtrays in Michael Barrymore's House? Cos he chucks all his fags in the pool.

Confucious he say...
Man with hole in pocket feel cocky all day

I hate crushing pills up and putting them in my Gran's dinner. I feel sneaky, but if I ever got her pregnant I wouldn't be able to forgive myself.

Matt Lucas's ex-partner hanged himself this week. Matt is said to be distraught but on a lighter note, he is now the only gay in the village.

A little girl walks into her parents' bedroom.
"Holy F**k" she screams "and YOU want ME to see a doctor about sucking my thumb!"

Wee Irish boy crying by the side of the road.
A man asks "What's wrong?"
Boy says "Me Ma is dead"
"Oh bejaysus" the man says "Do you want me to get Father O'Riley ?"
Wee boy replies "No thanks Mister, sex is the last ting on me moind roight now."

Once upon a time a guy asked a girl "Will you marry me?"
The girl said "No" and she lived happily ever after.
She went shopping, drank vodka with friends, always had
a clean house, never had to cook, had a wardrobe full of
shoes and bags, stayed skinny and was never farted upon.
The End.

Just had a call from a charity asking me to donate some
of my clothes to the starving people of the world.
I told them to "f**k off, anyone who fits into my clothes
isn't starving!"

Japanese scientists have now created a digital camera
with such a fast speed that it's now possible to take a
photograph of a woman with her gob shut.

Turned on my Sat Nav and it said 'Bear Left' and there was the zoo.
How good is that?

I hate all this terrorist business. I used to love the days
when you could look at an unattended bag on the train or
bus and think "I'm f**king having that!"

Man lost in a hot air balloon over Ireland. He looks down and sees
a farmer and shouts to him, "Where am I?"
The Irish farmer looks up and shouts back "You can't kid me ya

b'stard, you're in that feckin basket!"

Paddy is cleaning his rifle and accidentally shoots his
wife. He dials 999. Paddy says "It's my wife, I've accidentally shot
her. I've killed her"
Operator: "Please calm down sir. Can you first make sure she really
is dead?"
CLICK, BANG,
Paddy: "OK, done that, what next?

One day a man is walking along the beach and sees a quadriplegic
girl on the boardwalk, sitting in her wheelchair and crying.
He decides to be a good samaritan and asks her what's wrong.
She replies sadly, "I've never been hugged."
So he hugs the girl, which seems to cheer her up and he continues
on his way.
The next day he sees the girl again, still sitting on the boardwalk
and crying, so he asks her what's wrong and she replies, "I've never
been kissed."
So, he kisses the girl dutifully and goes on his way.
The following day, he passes her again, and once again, she's cry-
ing and he asks her what's wrong.
She replies, "I've never been screwed."
So, the man wheels her down the boardwalk, pushes her off the
pier and says, "Now, you're screwed!"

How do cripples make love? They rub their crutches together

A couple of tetraplegics go up to an ice cream van and ask, "can we
have a couple of 99's please?"
The ice cream man says, "certainly, would you like chocolate
sauce or strawberry sauce?"
One of the tetraplegics replies, "it doesn't really matter mate...
we're gonna to drop 'em anyway."

A man is walking down the street and sees a guy at a bus stop with
no arms or legs.

He calls to him, "hey mate, how are you getting on?"

I organised a day of sponsored bungee jumping for the local disabled group
Perhaps calling it 'splastics on elastic' wasn't my finest hour

So I've got a new girlfriend
She invited me around to her place for dinner the other night
We were in the kitchen, just about to start making dinner when she asked me to turn on the veg
Apparently, fingering her disabled daughter was not the right move...

Police today arrested a thalidomide couple at Heathrow airport
They were charged under the terrorism act, for trying to take small arms onto a plane

A boy who couldn't see, hear, smell, feel or taste punched me in the face yesterday
I told him there was no need for senseless violence

I should be ashamed of myself for making all these jokes at the expense of the disabled!
After all, they can't even stand up for themselves

I met a bloke in a wheelchair today, his face was battered and bruised
"What happened to your face?" I asked
"I am a Paralympian," he replied
"Boxing?" I enquired
"No..." He said, "... Hurdles"

What's got four wheels and flies?
A dead cripple

I was playing Scrabble and put down S-P-A-S-T-I-C
Got a cripple word score for that

EPILOGUE

To steal ideas from one is Plagiarism .... To steal from many is Research

Printed in Poland
by Amazon Fulfillment
Poland Sp. z o.o., Wrocław